Wandering Hearts

LOOKING GLASS SAGA

BOOK FOUR

Wandering Hearts

TANYA LISLE

SCRAP PAPER ENTERTAINMENT

ISBN-13: 978-1-988911-72-4

Scrap Paper Entertainment
www.scrappaperentertainment.com

Contents

CHAPTER 1

Winter Wonders

AFTER SIX HOURS on a plane and another half hour in a van with Adrianna and her brothers, Alice wasn't sure what she was expecting when they finally pulled up to Adrianna's house. The excitement of taking a plane for the first time had worn off by the first hour in the sky and she found herself anxious to be able to walk around without having to squeeze between other people. At this point, she would have taken just about anything that wasn't a small room that she had to share with several other bodies.

What she got was the Case house and it was huge. With a family of ten, they likely needed the space, but she hadn't expected to see the signs of people even as they drove up to it. There was a car up on blocks off to one side of the driveway, abandoned in the snow that had mostly been cleared. Someone had made a few snowmen and left large snow boulders in the front on the way to the house itself.

There was also a small house off to the side of the main one that looked like someone inhabited it. The curtains were not completely shut and, while the lights were off, Alice could tell that someone likely lived inside at some point. She wondered if that meant she was going to be meeting even more of Adrianna's family that had decided to visit.

Though Alice offered, she was shuffled into the house with Adrianna as her brothers dealt with their bags. She tried to stay out of the way, taking in the foyer with wide eyes. It felt warm, and not just because it was heated. Someone had bothered to decorate with Christmas decorations and that made it feel at least a little festive, whether they wanted it to be or not. It even smelled like pine.

"So you guys finally made it," an older man said, coming into the large foyer at the sound of the commotion. His chocolate brown hair looked shaggy and he had the same smile on his face as the rest of the family. Another one of Adrianna's brothers. "About damn time."

"Good to see you too," Travis said, dropping the bags at the door. "A little hand?"

The new brother proceeded to start clapping, procuring several rolled eyes as some of them went back out to the cars to get more bags.

"And you must be Addie's friend," the new brother said, stepping forward. "Alice, right? I'm Ryan. I'm sure everyone's told you plenty of lies about me already. So nice of you to join us this year. Now, where is that sister of mine?"

Adrianna reached out and smacked him lightly on the arm, looking a little annoyed. He smiled and picked her up in a hug, then put her back down. "Still in one piece?" he asked. "Haven't let Lance get away with anything too fun this semester, have you?"

"Like she could stop me," Mike said behind him. Alice was going to have to remember to call him Lance while she was here.

"Dad says they didn't even hear about you once," Ryan said. "How the hell did you manage that?"

"Adam and Matt weren't getting me into trouble," he said.

"So Evan had an easier job of covering for you?"

"Pretty much," Evan said, coming back in from the snow with the rest of the bags. "Let's hope the streak continues after I graduate."

"He's still got two more brothers to cover his ass," Ryan said, winking at Lance. "I'm sure he'll be fine."

Alice moved nervously out of the way, over to her bag, listening as the family talked around her. It wasn't just that she felt out of place amongst them and like she didn't know what she should be doing here, though that was certainly part of it. It was more how casual they sounded about two of their brothers being completely absent. A pang of guilt went through her as she shrank out of their way.

Adrianna found Alice's arm, bags in her other hand, and tugged her to the stairs. "Come on," she said. "I'll show you where you're going to be staying. There's a room right across from mine."

Alice followed her up, looking back as the brothers all seemed to devolve into playful bickering amongst one another, and she was glad to be out of it. With everyone seeming to want to talk to Ryan, she felt like she was intruding on a private moment, even if they were so loud that Alice could hear them as they went down the long hall and around the corner.

"This one's yours," Adrianna told her as she opened the first door around the corner and turned on the light to a bedroom. It was only a little smaller than Alice's back home, and even more sparsely decorated. It was blue and beige throughout and had a queen sized bed, a desk, and a dresser with a mirror on it. There were a few pictures of generic flowers hung up on the wall. On the far side of the room, there was an open door to a bathroom.

"My room's right there," Adrianna told her, indicating the room directly across from this one. "I'm going to take a shower. If you need anything, my door's usually open."

"Thanks," Alice said, not sure what else to say. Adrianna

went off into her own room, Alice staring after her. Adrianna didn't close the door behind her. Alice had a distinct sense of uneasiness about it. She took a step toward the door to close her own, but stopped herself. She should do what everyone else in the house did, and if they left the doors open, then she would do that too.

Instead, she moved out of the way of it, putting her bags down on the bed and taking a seat. After being cramped with other people for so long, the solitude was welcome, even if she didn't have the quiet. The house sounded like people, with voices drifting through the halls even as she heard the doors opening and closing. She couldn't even tell if any of the doors were the front door, and no one seemed to care about being loud. Already, she could hear the faint beat from one of the other rooms echoing through the halls. It was more like being back at school than home.

Except for the door.

With a deep breath, she got back to her feet. She was going to take a shower too. And if she did that, she would have to shut the door, right? Adrianna had done that, so it would be all right if she did the same. The door closed softly under her hands, bringing with it the quiet and a strange sight. There was a lock on the inside of it, like at school.

Ignoring the odd leap that her heart made in her chest, Alice went to the washroom and took a shower, cleaning off the day of travel she didn't realize she'd been so dirty with. She felt lighter as she changed into clean clothes from her bag and took the opportunity to look around the room a little better. It was very plain, but Alice didn't mind. It was the first time she had been allowed to stay with a friend, so she had no expectations of accommodations.

She stopped as she opened the drawer on the bedside table. The rest of the drawers and closet in the room had been empty, but there was a small package that had been left inside. She vaguely remembered once finding a book in a bedside table before, back when her family had taken a vacation, but this was nothing of the sort. It was a small box wrapped in red and green with a tag on it. Beneath it was an envelope with *Alice* written on it in handwriting that she had not seen in over a year.

Alice put the present back on the bedside table and went to the envelope, glad to find that it had not been sealed. She wasn't sure if she was allowed to open it yet and glanced at the door to make sure it was still closed before hastily opening the envelope and pulling out a card. There were no words on the front, just a bird with mistletoe, and she opened it.

Alice,

Merry Christmas. I'm sorry I missed last year, so I made you something special. Maybe leave these at school so Dad doesn't find them. Hope everything is going well and you're having fun at Lucena Academy. I miss you and I'm sorry I cannot be there.

Love Lori

Questions ran through her mind that she couldn't piece together. She wanted to know where her sister was and if she was all right and why she hadn't contacted her before now and how she'd gotten a card from England into her bedside table.

The knock at her door made her jump and she turned to stare at it, waiting for her father to catch her with the card. Instead, a voice came drifting through the door. "Alice, are you in there? Are you decent?"

Alice scrambled to hide the card quietly under the pillow. "I'm decent," she said, not moving from the bed.

The door cracked open and Joe peeked in. "How are you settling?" he asked. "Finding everything okay?"

Alice nodded. "Thank you."

"Dinner's ready downstairs. Addie's just getting ready and she'll be down in a bit if you want to wait for her."

"Okay. Thank you."

Joe smiled as his eyes drifted off of her and to the gift she left on the table. "If you have gifts, we can put them under the tree," he offered.

"I found it," Alice said, still confused. "It's for me. From Lori."

Alice didn't understand the look that flickered across Joe's face, but it returned to a gentle smile soon after. "Grab it and we'll still put it under the tree," he said. "Cards are fine, but we don't do gifts until Christmas Day. Come on," he added, tapping the door frame. "Dinner now. Sounds like Addie's done, too."

Alice nodded and got up, grabbing the present and giving it to Joe. Adrianna was there a moment later, hair in a wet braid down her back, and smiling. She went to Alice's side and, with a glance at Adrianna's room, Alice left her door open and followed the two of them down to dinner.

"What's that?" Adrianna asked, looking at the gift in Joe's hand.

"This is what we call a present," Joe teased her. "It's when one person gives another person something they think they would like, but makes them wait to figure out what it is and actually use it. It's a very ancient practice."

Alice stayed quiet as Adrianna frowned up at him, anxious about the card she'd left behind. Joe had said they were okay, but any note from Lori suddenly felt like contraband. After the way her parents had declined to even mention her sister, she wasn't sure if she should have told Joe about the present. If her father found out...

"Come on," Adrianna said, snapping Alice out of her reverie. They were in a room with a very large table and several of Adrianna's brothers already sitting at it. They looked different than they did at school, clearly more comfortable here, even if comfortable for Joe meant that he looked a bit like he'd just walked out of a cartoon that Alice would get in trouble for watching. She followed Adrianna to a spot near the end by a man who must be Adrianna's father.

"So this is Alice," he said as Alice took a seat, offering a hand. Alice shook it and he smiled before letting her go. "I have heard a great deal about you," he said. "All of it good." A look crossed his face, though Alice knew what he meant. He spoke to Alice's father, who had a rather interesting opinion of Alice to say the least.

"It's a pleasure to meet you," she said. Her father would likely be checking in to make sure she was on her best behaviour and she had no intent to give Mr. Case any reason to tell him anything. "You have a lovely home."

"Not so lovely kids filling it, though," he said, smiling back at the kids sitting at the table. "Unfortunately, Claudia isn't feeling too well tonight, though I think she just wanted to miss the madness of the kids getting home. She should be up again tomorrow, though. Not to worry. Addie, maybe grab Alice a plate?"

Adrianna got up and went to the kitchen, leaving Alice

alone at the table with her father. Alice's smile became set as she realized what was coming. She looked around, finding that at least Lance was nearby, sitting just across from her and occasionally glancing over when she wasn't staring at the door, so perhaps the interrogation from Mr. Case wouldn't be too bad.

"So how was the flight?" Mr. Case asked her. "I hear it was your first time on a plane."

"It was good," Alice said.

"And the boys haven't been giving you any trouble, have they?" His eyes glanced over to Lance, who very abruptly looked back to the door.

"No, they've been fine."

He laughed at that. "That's a word I haven't heard used for them in a while," he told her. "They're usually a bit of a pain collectively. I got a call about some of them pushing you into a lake."

"It was fine," Alice said. Adrianna had chosen that moment to come back with two plates of spaghetti in her hands. She set one down in front of Alice and Alice was glad to have a reason to be free of the conversation.

"Is Rayne here?" Lance asked, looking pointedly at his father. Alice knew that look, like he was asking something else entirely that he didn't want to say. Beside him, Travis straightened up and started to pay attention. "She should be here."

"No," their father said. "She's staying with friends for the holidays."

"Rayne?" Alice asked quietly, turning to Adrianna.

"Oh, she's kind of like our housekeeper," Adrianna told her. "She lives in the house next to ours and helps clean up stuff. But only sometimes. She's usually studying and working on stuff for Claudia. You'd really like her. She's a lot of fun."

Lance didn't look happy with the answer, "She's also—"

"Which friends?" Travis asked over him, shooting Lance a warning look. A look of pain crossed Lance's face before he forced it into an almost sarcastic smile. "I don't think she mentioned that."

"I believe she said it was Jackie," their father said. "She might be back around New Year's."

"Probably not," Lance muttered. Travis shot him another sharp look, but he said nothing else, stuffing his mouth full of spaghetti.

Alice wasn't used to dinner like the Cases did it. There were conversations, vibrant ones that moved up and down the table, spoken between mouthfuls. Alice stayed silent for it, watching and listening as Ryan and Evan started talking about various schools that Evan was planning to apply to in the next year. Near her, Mr. Case was paying Lance a little attention.

"I think this is the quietest the phone has ever been while you kids were at school," he said. He glanced at Alice and gave her a grin. "First it was these two," he said, indicating Joe and Travis, "but as soon as they stopped being little hellions, the next batch went in."

"There is no way we were as bad as these three," Joe said.

"Just because you two didn't work together didn't mean I didn't get the same number of calls back from the school. I was worried they weren't going to let me dump them or Addie in there at all after you two."

"We are not that bad!" Lance insisted. "It's just a couple little harmless things here and there. Nothing permanent. It can all get cleaned up in under an hour. It's not like we ever spray-painted a car, *Travis*."

"One time."

"I can't even believe they let you back in after that."

"Unlike the three that changed all the locks on the dorms on day one," Joe said. "And don't think we didn't know who did it. You three are always a pain in the ass about it all. It's kind of nice with just one of you around now."

Alice felt a pang of guilt at that, but she let it fall. While she was here, she was going to try and not go off into Wonderland to find Mark — Adam while she was here — and Matt. It seemed like a bad idea with too many people who might find out. While she was in school they had a door that locked and people weren't trying to find her all the time. Here, Alice was sure people were going to be keeping track of her much more closely. She would have to be a lot more careful about her trips to Wonderland so she didn't get caught.

Adrianna nudged Alice gently to get her attention. "You wanna go shopping tomorrow?" Adrianna asked. "I have to get stuff for everyone. And figure out what everyone wants. You haven't done anything yet either, right?"

Alice shook her head. She hadn't even thought about Christmas shopping yet and it hadn't actually occurred to her that she would need to do it. For as long as she could remember, either her mother or Ms. Miller had taken care of that for her. On occasion, she would be brought to a store and be allowed to point out the things she wanted to get for people but, as she looked around the table, she realized that there were a lot of people she now had to shop for and no guiding hand to tell her what she should be getting in case she chose wrong.

"Maybe we should wait a couple days," Joe suggested. "Get settled and let the Christmas greed seep in a little more so we have something to try and work from when we try to get everything."

"Christmas greed is good," Lance said. "I'm all for letting a little Christmas greed give me an easier time to figure out what to get everyone. Even if everything's just getting mailed here in a week already gift wrapped."

"Aw, no fair!" Adrianna said. "You're done already?"

Lance grinned. "Online shopping," he said. "You'll figure it out one of these days."

Alice kept quiet, smiling and laughing at the appropriate moments. The conversation drifted again, to different traditions and things they did in the season, then to plans they needed to make. Alice kept nodding and trying not to feel like she was in over her head. She didn't know what she was supposed to do here. This was not like her home or like school. She didn't know what the rules were here, and she could tell Mr. Case would not be telling her what she needed to do.

She spotted a flash of purple in her fork and a wicked grin that almost seemed like it was taunting her with somewhere where she knew exactly what she needed to do. Maybe just one trip into Wonderland while she was here. She had to find Adrianna's brothers still, after all.

CHAPTER 2

Deals Made

ALICE WAS ALREADY awake when the knock at her door came early the next morning. "Come in," she said, unsure if she was supposed to be out of bed at all, much less going through her things and trying to decide if she should be unpacking for her holiday stay.

Adrianna let herself in, smiling brightly and still dressed in her pajamas. "Morning!" she said, setting herself down on the bed. "How did you sleep?"

"Good. It's nice in here."

"I wanted you to stay in my room, but dad said you might want your own space after sharing a room with me all year." Adrianna smiled and Alice knew she didn't mean to imply anything by that. "I think Claudia wants to take us shopping today."

"Your stepmom, right?"

Adrianna nodded. "She's probably already downstairs if you want to meet her too."

Alice looked over her luggage and then back to Adrianna. "Sure," she said. "I can just get changed."

"Why? We're on holiday."

"Right. Okay."

Alice followed Adrianna down to the kitchen, the noise of the house hitting her as soon as she walked out of her room. It wasn't loud, but it felt more like school than it did like home. People were very clearly here, and they didn't bother keeping their music or their chatter quiet. As they drew closer to the kitchen, it only got louder, as it seemed more of the family was already up and about.

Claudia Case was very easy to spot, and not just because she was the only older woman Alice had seen since entering the house. For a stepmother, she looked just like the rest of the family, fitting the look of them with a strangely unsettling perfection. Her long dark hair was tied loosely behind her and she took in a leisurely mug of something that looked too red to be coffee. Alice thought she looked a little too much like an older version of Adrianna for her to have just been a stepmother.

Ryan tended to the dishes in the sink, nodding to the girls before turning back to his chores.

Claudia saw the pair of them as soon as Alice spotted

her. "Alice, I presume," she said, smiling at her. There was something almost regal about her, and Alice could feel herself straightening to greet her.

"Hello, Mrs. Case," Alice said. "I heard you weren't feeling well last night. Are you alright today?"

"Oh my, what a sweet girl you are," she said. "No wonder Adrianna's taken a liking to you."

"Thank you," Alice said.

"Now, your mother has sent over a few things for you," Claudia Case said, taking a small box off the counter beside her and handing it to Alice. "There's a tree in the living room if anything is a gift. We try not to open anything until the twenty-fifth." She eyed Ryan, who smiled back in that innocent way that Lance did when he knew he was in trouble. As all of the boys did when they knew they were in trouble, she noticed.

Claudia handed Alice a butter knife and got to her feet to fetch both her and Adrianna a bowl of cereal. Alice took the knife uneasily and carefully opened the expedited parcel. She got it open just as Claudia returned, sliding the cereal onto the counter and out of the way. Inside was a small wallet with a few cards and slips of paper in it, along with a small gift.

"Well, one of those is for the tree," Claudia said, whipping it out from Alice's hands, continuing to the living room and out of sight. Adrianna leaned in to look at the wallet Alice had gotten. It looked like it had been used, but Alice didn't recognize it or the card inside. It was a Visa from the looks of it, with a note that told her there was $500 on the card.

"I guess I can go shopping now," Alice said.

"I'll ask Claudia if we're actually going today," Adrianna said. She hurried off into the next room, leaving Alice with the cereal and Ryan at the sink. Alice started to eat quietly, waiting for Adrianna to get back, and glanced up to Ryan.

Ryan certainly seemed nice enough so far. He went to school somewhere out of state and came back for the breaks, from what Adrianna had mentioned about him before. He also had a tendency to treat her like a kid a lot, though Alice thought it might be because Adrianna was the youngest of them all. Other than that, she really didn't know much about him and didn't really know if she needed to know that much. She already had so many other brothers to keep track of and they'd lost two of them as it was. And even with two missing, there were still a lot of brothers.

"How are you liking it here so far?" Ryan asked.

Alice snapped up and hoped that he hadn't been talking to her this whole time without her paying attention. He was looking at her with the same, slightly concerned eyes as Adrianna. "It's nice," Alice said, not really sure what to say. "Your house is really big."

Ryan laughed. "That's what everyone says," he told her.

"Takes people a while to get used to it. You're doing fine, though," he added, offering her a grin before going back to a particularly difficult pot.

"Thank you?" Alice said, though she wasn't sure how she was supposed to take that.

Ryan laughed again. "So polite. And I hear you've been getting into trouble with Lance and them. I don't suppose you know where Adam and Matt — Oh, sorry, *Mark* and Matt — I swear those three had better drop that soon. Don't suppose you know where the two of them have gone and run off to? Lance is giving me nothing."

Alice shook her head, though her heart leapt in her chest. "I'm sorry." Her voice stayed even. "Adrianna and Lance say they're going to turn up, though."

"Yeah, turn up," he said, his eyes clouding over at the words. Alice wondered if she was imagining it, or if he was washing that pot a lot more slowly than he had been a moment ago.

She looked back to see Adrianna with Claudia in tow. Looking at her now, Alice was starting to get a weird feeling about Claudia. She seemed to fit a little too well in here, somehow, and it seemed wrong. Alice didn't understand why she had only just now noticed it, but that suspicion started to fade away as the sound of Ryan cleaning picked up again. Alice did her best not to let her expression change, but she was sure that something had just happened.

"We are!" Adrianna said, positively excited for it. "Later this afternoon, though."

"No need to go so early," Claudia told them. "Ryan, did you want to come?"

"I'm done," Ryan said, his mind completely off his missing brothers again. Alice wondered if he still remembered that they were even missing, or if he was concerned about it anymore. For a moment, she glanced at Adrianna and wondered if she remembered. Evan remembered, after all, so maybe...

Right, Evan. She needed those photos from him. Evan still had the entire brown book on his phone. In the time since she had given that up, she hadn't asked him about it and she hoped he didn't delete it off of there yet. She desperately hoped he still had it. She could dimly remember pages here and there from the missing month, but if he still had it, then maybe there was still some hope.

The month itself was such a strange jumble of memories. She was so out of it that she couldn't really grasp any of them properly. The memories of Tiger Lily and her imprisonment lay underneath another layer of far more clear and generalized memories of going through life and doing regular school things. There was absolutely nothing specific in there, just a generic bunch of experiences she could have had at any time at school, along with enough information so that she could pass her exams well enough to not arouse suspicion. If she thought hard, she could still remember what actually happened, but they were not memories that she wanted to relive.

"Are you okay?" Adrianna asked her quietly.

Alice realized she must have been staring off into space and smiled. "I'm fine," she said. "I was just thinking. About that month, you know?"

Adrianna understood. "Have you gotten the pictures off of Evan yet?" she asked.

Alice shook her head and Adrianna started to lead her through the house. "Come on," she said, leading Alice back upstairs. Though the doors were not decorated, Adrianna seemed to know exactly who was behind each of them and led Alice purposefully down the hall. "I think he'll be awake by now. It's not that early."

They stopped at one of the many doors along the hall and knocked. They waited a moment, Alice shifting nervously as she waited for the answer. Her mind was racing with possibilities and she worried that this was a bad idea. She didn't know if Evan even remembered that she was missing that month or knew what those photos on his phone even were. He might have deleted them already. He might have forgotten that she was gone in the first place and think she'd gone crazy. If her father found out that she had said or done something that might seem off while she was at Adrianna's house, she'd probably get shipped back to her locked room, if not to another doctor, immediately.

With no answer, Adrianna knocked harder. "Evan?" she called inside.

There was a scrambling and then Evan came to the door, hair a mess and still in his pajamas. "Addie?" Evan asked, wiping his eyes clear from the sleep still in them. "What time is it?"

"Ten," she said. "I'm sorry. Were you sleeping?"

"It's fine," he said. "What did you want?"

"You have Alice's pictures still," she said.

Evan wiped at his eyes and looked beside Adrianna to see Alice. "Right," he said, running a hand through his hair and opening the door to let them in. He stifled a yawn. "Come in," he said.

Alice followed Adrianna into Evan's room. The walls were sparsely decorated with his own accomplishments. There were awards and medals up on one wall, but the only other thing he had on them were a couple shelves with books. There were clothes left on the foot of his bed, but most of his living was clearly done at the computer, where papers were scattered and notes were strewn about, held down under a mug.

He went back to his bed and the table beside it where

he kept his phone. Though he was clearly not awake yet, he threw on his glasses before picking up his phone and sat down on the bed. His attention stayed on the screen as he went through it. A few taps and his look soured.

"You aren't going to like this," he said, passing the phone to Alice.

"So you remember what happened?" Alice asked, almost scared to know the answer. She didn't want to hear that he was looking for something else on his phone, but she took it from his hands anyway and began to look through the photos.

"Mostly," he said. "Someone else from my year went missing, too, but no one else seems to have noticed. And then someone else started getting really good with chemistry. I'm pretty sure I'm the only one who realizes that Sally's gone at all, though, so I just keep trying to not think about it. And there were the other people in that garden, but no one's mentioned anything about the rest of them yet."

"I'm sorry," Alice said, looking down through photos on the phone. Her face fell too, as did Adrianna's who was looking over her shoulder. She went through the photos one by one, but each of them was distorted and changed. She could still kind of make them out, but it was like the photos had been cut up into little squares and then squares were thrown randomly back onto the screen. "What happened?"

"No idea," Evan said. "Sorry. I can still send them to you if you want them, but I don't know how they got like that."

"I have some idea," Alice said, more depressed than suspicious. The Bandersnatch was not an idiot. He probably knew what she was doing and decided that this was cheating, so he made it difficult for her to continue to use the book like she was planning. It *was* cheating when she really thought about it, but she didn't have any other option if she wanted a chance against him.

She couldn't let herself get upset, though. She needed to think of something else, but for now she would try to work out as much as she could from the scrambled photos. Maybe if she looked at them long enough, she would remember what was in them on her own "I'll still take them, if you don't mind," she said. "I'll figure out how to read them later."

"Sooner's a good idea," Evan said, taking his phone back. "Or come up with something else that might work. Cheat if you have to. You don't have much time left. And when it's gone, well, who knows who he's going to let remember you, right?"

"Evan!" Adrianna snapped.

Evan didn't look at either of them, instead plugging the phone into the computer and starting to get the photos off of it. He didn't seem like he was quite done with asking questions yet, though he wasn't saying anything as he worked. His fingers moved swiftly over the keys for a minute before he stopped, staring at the screen and starting to move through the windows to type on another one.

"Any luck finding Adam or Matt yet?" he asked. Alice felt like she was talking to a teacher who wanted to know why she hadn't turned in an assignment yet instead of Adrianna's slowly awakening brother, though she knew this was likely what he wanted to ask in the first place. The question would have been a relief if she had better news.

Alice shook her head. "I thought I saw one of them while we were still at school, but I couldn't get back through. Part of the deal. But I think one of them at least probably talked to the Hatter like Lance did before. Everyone ends up talking to the Hatter when they go into the forest at some point. You can't escape the tea party. And if he did, then he might still be trapped there when I go back."

"Take the holidays off from looking," Evan told her. He turned to look her in the eye.

Alice shrank under his gaze, but met it and said nothing, waiting.

"When you start going back, you're probably going to have to deal with that girl, right? I think her name was Tiger Belle or something?"

"Tiger Lily? How do you know about her?"

"There's a reason we never tell Addie anything," Evan said, turning back to the computer as it beeped at him.

"Hey, I can keep a secret!"

"Tiger Lily's probably not going to be too happy you slipped out while she was right outside," Evan said, making a little too much sense as he went back to staring at the screen and typing madly once more. "And she's been able to catch you twice. She knows how to keep you there now, and we can't get you out from this side. And your father is very happy to call lawyers if we lose you here. I am not spending any of my vacation dealing with those if I can help it."

"Okay," Alice said. It made sense and she didn't want to do anything to get Adrianna or her family in trouble while she was here.

Beside her, Adrianna was already getting up to go and Alice followed.

"And you'd never get away with disappearing around here," he added as she got to the door. "There's way too many of us and everyone's always checking in on each other. You disappear and people will notice."

"Yeah," Alice agreed. "I thought so."

Adrianna pulled her out of the room and back into the hall, rolling her eyes and pulling her along. "Don't listen to him," Adrianna told her. "He's always grumpy when he wakes up. He doesn't remember how to be nice until after he gets caffeine."

Alice smiled and let the whole matter go. "I wasn't going to go anyway," she said. "I didn't want to get stuck there again and make you and Evan and Lance worry about me again. But I do want to get them back, Adrianna. I need to."

"It's okay," Adrianna said. "We'll be too busy for you to head over there anyway."

CHAPTER 3

Mrs. Claudia Case

ADRIANNA GAVE ALICE a full tour of the house. It wasn't as difficult to navigate as Alice worried, but there were a lot of places in it that looked like they weren't used that often. One whole hall was just for Claudia to use for work, though Adrianna couldn't say what it was she did. The tour ended in the foyer, where they met Joe and Travis and, as a family, they piled into the minivan to head to the mall with Mrs. Case.

Alice wasn't sure what to make of Mrs. Case. Claudia, as she insisted on being called. She drove them around, but she kept Adrianna and Alice close while Joe and Travis went off in different directions, with instructions to call should anything go wrong. She smiled and said something about girl time, though Alice wasn't sure what that meant as the boys wandered off, leaving her and Adrianna with Claudia.

"So where do you girls want to go?" Claudia asked. "Who are we looking for stuff for?"

Adrianna led the way, apparently very comfortable with shopping and the mall. Claudia had no problem following her and Alice trailed behind, trying to think of something to get for everyone. There were so many people to buy for. She needed to get something for her mother and father, definitely, but she'd also need to find something for Mr. and Mrs. Case as well. She would need to get something for Adrianna and all of her brothers, just to be polite, but she didn't know what she was going to get for any of them.

And Lori. Lori had gotten her something. Should she get something for her as well? Did she even have a way of getting it to her?

Luckily for her, Adrianna was well versed in her brothers and finding gifts. She went through the mall, picking out something sisterly for herself to give to her brothers, and then something more appropriate for Alice to get them as a guest as well. Alice was grateful for her being there, but it was exhausting watching her go through the stores and picking things out. Occasionally, Adrianna would ask Alice for her opinion on something, but Alice was too lost to know what to say.

Claudia had her moments as well. She called for a break and a quick snack right when Alice thought she was going to collapse from all this walking around with bags. Claudia took everything from their arms and brought them to the gift wrapping. She covered the cost of getting them wrapped while they took the time to get some ice cream to celebrate everything finally being done, and all in one very long afternoon.

"The bubble gum here is pretty good," Claudia said, seeing that Alice was taking her time choosing between the flavours. "The corn is a little weird, though."

"Corn?" Alice asked, following her finger. Sure enough, down at the end nestled amongst a lot of strange flavours was one labeled *corn*. Alice stared at it for a minute, not really sure what to make of it.

"I don't know why either," she said. "It seems like a strange choice."

Alice ordered the bubble gum on Claudia's recommendation and joined Adrianna while Claudia ordered something for herself. She plopped down into the seat across from her, exhausted and looking around at all the places they'd been to already, a little worried that they weren't done yet. "This place is really big," Alice said, starting in on her ice cream very slowly. Everything around here was really big, but the mall was another beast entirely. If she was going to go back out there, she wanted time for her feet to stop hurting first.

"It's not that big," Adrianna said. "There's one that's as big as a whole city!"

Alice was not as excited about the idea as she was. "We aren't going to that one, are we?" Alice asked, already terrified for her feet. She wished she were wearing her gym shoes.

"No," Claudia said, joining them. "It's a little far from here, and I don't think we could get your parents' permission to bring you over the border just to go shopping."

Alice was safe for now. The idea of walking around an even bigger mall than this trying to pick out gifts for people she didn't know well enough to go shopping for was nightmarish. As it was, she had never had so much input on what she bought before today. She wasn't usually asked for her opinion very often before now, but Ms. Miller could never coax one out of her like Adrianna could.

"So Alice," Claudia said, turning and smiling down at her. "Addie has told me so much about you already."

"Claudia," Adrianna said, embarrassment showing in her voice and on her face.

"But you've been so quiet today," she continued as if Adrianna had said nothing. "It's okay, you know. I won't bite."

"I'm sorry," Alice said, trying to smile. It was a very awkward conversation to have with an adult, even if she was trying to make her feel better. It was even stranger to have a conversation with an adult who looked like an adult version of her friend. "I just... I don't really go shopping much at home.

Mom doesn't really take me with her much. And this mall is so big. I don't really know what I'm doing here."

Claudia was sympathetic when she smiled. "Then it's a good thing that we're just about done. I think Adrianna just wanted to get one last thing before we head out." She gave Adrianna a meaningful look as Adrianna finished her ice cream and she scrambled off into the mall, leaving Alice alone with Claudia.

Alice started to get up, though her cup of ice cream was still half full. "I should—"

Claudia reached over and grabbed her forearm, urging her to sit back down. Alice looked down at Claudia's hand, feeling something strange coming from her fingers and spreading up Alice's arm. It was a strange feeling, both warm and cold at once that enveloped her and felt like it was trying to seep into her. While she sat down, she tensed up, which seemed to be enough to keep the feeling from getting in through her skin and into her insides.

She looked at Claudia, who met her eyes and pulled her hand away with a cool smile. Alice didn't know what she did, but Claudia seemed to be aware that whatever it was not only hadn't worked, but Alice also knew about it. She stayed very still in her seat and neither of them looked away, both unsure how to proceed. Alice wasn't even sure what Claudia was trying to do, or what she even could do. She shouldn't be able to do anything at all. This wasn't Wonderland. Even if it were Wonderland, she'd never felt anything quite like that before.

"Addie's looking for something for *you*, dear," Claudia said after a moment. "She wouldn't want you seeing what it was before Christmas."

It was like nothing had happened at all and Alice was willing to let it stay that way for now. There were a lot of people in the food court with them and she didn't want to cause a scene. She settled back into her ice cream, though she felt nervous about being left alone with her now. "Oh," Alice said, shifting in her seat and moving away from Claudia. "I should find something for her too, then."

"You already did," Claudia pointed out. "You asked her if she'd like it before you got it, remember? Right near the start."

"Right," Alice said. She had already forgotten the first store they went in amidst the sea of what seemed like thousands they'd been through. She could remember Sarah and Heather talking about shopping before at one point, and they were happy enough to spend hours inside of a mall if they were given the chance, but it left Alice feeling exhausted and barely able to keep track of anything that had happened. She wouldn't be surprised if she got back to Adrianna's house and realized that Claudia had done nothing at all to her and it was all just in her head.

"You're a very interesting girl, Alice," Claudia said, looking her over carefully from atop her folded hands. "Where did you say you were from again?"

"Seattle," Alice said, knowing that it wasn't what she was really asking. She felt like she was back in one of the doctor's offices and talking to one of the ones that her father had specifically chosen for her instead of the one that was recommended. Claudia's eyes looked her over and she was smiling like she was friendly, but those eyes were looking for a chink in her armour that she could pry wide open. It was something Alice was well versed in, and she stayed perfectly calm as Claudia decided to examine her.

"Nice place," she said. "I haven't been myself, but your sister has told me a lot about it. Rain, but nice summers, is that right?"

"Yes." Alice took another spoon of ice cream and ate it slowly. She was running out, but she hoped that Adrianna would be back soon.

"Have you ever travelled?" Claudia asked. It was an oddly specific question, Alice had to admit, for someone looking for a chink. Still, she didn't react any more than to finish off her spoon of ice cream. She met Claudia's eyes as she continued. "Maybe took a nice vacation somewhere exotic and completely out of this world? Some place that was maybe a little magical, almost?"

Now Alice felt like she was talking to the doctors again,

who were always trying to make her talk about Wonderland and then would tell her that she was crazy for having ever brought it up. And then they'd give her the pills to make her stop feeling anything.

"No," Alice said, looking a little curious as she did so. She knew how to play this game well now. "You mean like Disneyland? I've always wanted to go visit there. My parents haven't taken me yet, but they keep saying they might one day."

Claudia grinned that cruel grin of a doctor that knew she was being played. "Not quite what I was thinking."

"I don't really know many other places in North America that might be kind of magical," Alice said. "Unless you mean somewhere farther. I only just took a plane for the first time yesterday, though."

"You're an interesting girl, Alice," she said again, seeming to accept this for now.

Adrianna returned, smiling and sitting back down. "All done!" she said triumphantly. She turned back to Claudia, looking a little distressed. "But they have so much stuff at the gift wrapping place. They said it was going to be a few hours until they were going to be done with everything."

"I can come back tomorrow and get everything," Claudia assured her. I think five hours is quite long enough for all of us to spend in a mall at any time, don't you? Can you text Joe and see if they want a ride home? I think I saw them meeting up with friends earlier."

Adrianna conceded to that and Alice was grateful that they were leaving. The crowds of people were more than Alice had ever seen in one place at a time and she wasn't used to walking around and shopping as much as Adrianna was. She remembered seeing shows when Lori managed to show her anything unsupervised and seeing how the girls all loved the mall, but after Christmas shopping, she was exhausted and didn't want to do it ever again.

She was glad when they headed home, carrying none of their spoils, and Alice dropped down on the couch as soon as she could. The footrest popped up so she could put her feet up. Adrianna took a seat on the seat next to her and did the same, picking up the remote and turning on the television to the first Christmas special that she could find. Alice glanced around to make sure Adrianna's father wasn't here to tell Alice's father that she was watching what looked like a very strange cartoon that Alice would never have been allowed to watch at home.

Apparently Santa Claus, whom Alice was aware of but never really knew much about, was a child who was raised by fairies and was sometimes attacked by monsters. Somehow, this was not in line at all with any of the things that Alice had grown up learning about the figure. They were joined by Ryan, who was quick to point out how completely inaccurate the fairies were, as well as the creatures that they were fighting against. He seemed to have an almost encyclopedic knowledge of the mythology of Santa Claus, but he used it to make the movie more entertaining and educational.

With Ryan there, she thought back to the morning when he was asking about his brothers. Clearly he remembered them, and sometimes the Case family even worried a little about what had happened to both of them. The times that had happened were fleeting, but it was enough to remind Alice that she really should be looking for them. It would be, if nothing else, a nice Christmas present if she could bring at least one of them back. And she had spotted one of them in Wonderland only recently.

When another Christmas movie started, this time a clay animation one about Rudolph, Santa's reindeer with the strange nose, and an elf that wanted something more out of life, Alice looked around for something reflective. She picked up a coaster, one with a reflective middle. With her head toward the screen, she looked down into the mirror and kept an eye on the room around her, just in case she would need to stop. She was only going to look.

Wonderland appeared in the coaster, starting at the Mad Hatter's tea party. The Jabberwocky was gone, but the Hatter seemed to have moved on, instead speaking passionately to a small group that seemed to be nodding politely. A few of them were even sipping their tea at the tea party.

Something might be very wrong in Wonderland.

Still, there was no sign of one of the Case boys sitting at the table, so she moved on. Next she checked the plain where Tiger Lily's tribe had set up. It was still there and the tent they had kept her in was empty. It was a good sign, really, though she wished she could look into the other tents. The mirror seemed reserved only for places where the Cheshire Cat wanted to bother her from and places she'd already been. Luckily, she had been across Wonderland at this point and there were no shortage of places to check.

The White Rabbit's house was empty. The Caterpillar was speaking to someone who was not a boy at all. The ruins of the Duchess' castle were still simply ruins with even fewer inhabitants. Everywhere she looked, there was nothing there that indicated that it was anything out of the ordinary for Wonderland, and no sign of a stranger that had been through there. Still, she'd seen someone that looked a lot like one of them falling through the sky before she left Lucena Academy. One of them was there and she knew it.

Though she moved through the parts of Wonderland, playing a large scale *Where's Waldo,* she didn't see him. Instead, there was something else strange there, even for Wonderland. There were people, animals and other beings just wandering around, heartless with those lifeless eyes staring at nothing. Alice didn't know what to make of it until she noticed that one of them was holding something. There was a fox, wandering through a path on a bridge going over a creek all on his own. He carried in his hands something that moved. A heart.

As soon as she recognized what it was, Alice slammed the coaster down on her lap and looked around to see if anyone had seen what she did. Joe and Evan had joined them in watching the movie, though they were too busy making fun of it to have noticed Alice did anything.

Alice knew someone had seen her. She could feel the eyes watching her from somewhere in the room. She looked back, finding Claudia walking through the hall that the doorway led to. On her other side, Lance had taken a seat in the chair and was watching her. He gave her an odd little nod before he turned his attention back to the television.

CHAPTER 4

Christmas Time

THERE WAS NO routine at the Case house during the holidays. Things just kept happening, and Alice wasn't sure what to make of it. Besides going to sleep and waking up at roughly the same time, there was no pattern. Meals were had scattered throughout the day with clusters of people, with only dinner being a family event, and even that happening at different times. She tried to just go with it, but it was strange not to have a pattern to follow.

Adrianna was at her side the whole time, urging her to join in with the rest of the family as they did all of the things their family did for the holidays. She baked cookies, built snowmen, helped decorate the house, and watched a lot of television. She even got to play a few video games, finding that she was decent at fighting games if she could hit all of the buttons faster than anyone else, and if she didn't play against

Joe or Lance. Travis was apparently pretty good as well, or so they told her, but he wasn't around very much.

Despite the fun of it, Alice knew she was being watched. Adrianna kept close to her, and she often caught Evan and Lance glancing in her direction as well. Claudia hadn't done anything as strange as she had on that day in the mall, though she did make an effort to say hello to Alice whenever they were in the same room together and have at least a few nice words to add to that.

There was an electricity building in the house as the tree continued to fill until Christmas Eve. She was told late in the day that they would be attending Midnight Mass and she was welcome to come if she wanted. Not looking forward to spending the night alone in a house other than her own, she gladly joined them.

Though she had never been to a Midnight Mass before, it wasn't that bad. Sure, she was tired and she didn't know any of the songs, when to sit, when to stand, or anything else, but there was a nice feeling of community in here that she'd never imagined from what Lori told her about church.

Alice tried to follow along as best she could, but she hadn't been to anything like this since she was very little. At least she wasn't the only one that was a little lost. It looked like very few people here seemed to be familiar with the movements.

When they got home, Alice went right to bed. It was a

lot later than she was used to and she was anxious about the morning. This was going to be a Christmas like she had never experienced before, much like the rest of the break had been so far. While tonight had been mostly preparing to go to Mass and everything had been simple, she got the feeling that the Cases celebrated Christmas because they genuinely enjoyed it rather than out of some sense of obligation.

Alice was awoken the next morning by a knock at her door. It was far earlier than she'd ever been up on Christmas before and she tried to ignore it, but the knocking wasn't going away. Gradually, she rolled out of bed and trudged to the door, mumbling something loudly enough to let the person knocking know she was coming.

"Alice!" Adrianna called from the other side of the door. "Alice, it's Christmas!"

Alice opened her door, bleary eyed and wavering on her feet. She wiped at her eye with her whole palm and looked at her. "Morning," she said, not at all sure why Adrianna looked so cheerful or completely awake this early in the morning. Even if it was Christmas, they couldn't do anything until everyone else was awake.

"Merry Christmas! Come on!"

Alice wasn't sure what she meant. Come on where? She was still half asleep and at the very least needed to pee before she went ahead and went anywhere. She muttered something, leaving Adrianna sitting on her bed as Alice made it into the washroom. She got some water on her face in an attempt to wake up, though she was still very tired.

When she looked up in the mirror, a pair of giant purple eyes were on her.

"Hello, Alice. Have you been peeping into Wonderland without me?"

Alice was suddenly very awake, looking back at the Cheshire Cat through the mirror. He was so close, and her mind went blank. Peeping? Did he see her looking into Wonderland? Had he been watching her?

"Alice?" Adrianna called from outside the door.

Alice forced the mirror to go back to reflecting only the washroom and left, her heart pounding in her chest. She knew she was going to have to be careful about being caught looking into Wonderland, but it hadn't really hit her that Wonderland would be looking back until just now. She needed to start keeping an eye on anything reflective from now on. Fantastic. Just what she wanted.

"I thought I heard something," Adrianna said when Alice came out.

"I'll tell you later," Alice said, not wanting to ruin her morning. She looked so happy that it was Christmas, and Alice tried to calm down enough to handle whatever Christmas the Cases had prepared for her. She could deal with Cat later.

She followed Adrianna downstairs to find that everyone was already awake. Evan even looked friendly this morning, smiling with his glasses on and his hair not sticking up in every random direction it could manage. None of them had gotten dressed, which was normal for some of them, and Joe hadn't even bothered to style his hair. He looked like he did in school, though she was sure it was only a matter of time before the spikes would come back.

It was already a lot different than any Christmas Alice had ever had. For one thing, Alice was up early. For another, they seemed to have a system to wake up their parents, since both their father and Claudia were up and dressed. They sat by the fire, watching the chaos of the kids organize themselves until the chaos transformed into something manageable.

Something manageable turned out to be a game of ones and twos to figure out an order for opening gifts, which they did before breakfast. It took Alice a bit to figure out how the game worked, eventually finding herself near the middle out of sheer luck and still not quite knowing what was going on. Like everything else that happened, she tried to just go with it, smiling and letting the Cases show her the way.

They went one by one through the pile, everyone waiting their turn more patiently than Alice expected given the group, and they seemed a lot more anxious to see someone open their gift than get one for themselves. Stranger still, Alice was surprised by how much she ended up getting from everyone, consisting of a lot of books and movies she had yet to read or see, as well as a new notebook from Adrianna.

It was surprising how much the Case family seemed to actually want to spend time with one another and Alice was trying very hard not to look shocked at that. She was happy for them, sure, but she didn't know how to react to it. She was even less sure of how to react when someone thanked her for getting them something.

She was waiting for one particular red and green package to come her way, and she was almost glad when everyone seemed too busy to pay attention to her when it finally arrived. A box addressed to her from Lori. Only Joe gave her a second look, nudging Travis and saying nothing as Alice was left to open it. Travis looked unhappy about it, but something else was shoved at him to distract him.

Alice carefully opened the gift from the bits of tape that held the wrapping on before opening the box. Inside was a set of jewelry made of delicate wirework that looked like small silver leaves with blue gems woven throughout them. There were earrings, a necklace, and even a bracelet, along with a couple clips for her hair. She knew the work immediately, knew that Lori had made it herself, and Alice wasn't sure how to react.

"Those are pretty," Adrianna said, looking over at them with a wide smile on her face. "Who got them for you?"

"Lori," Alice told her. In the end, she hadn't gotten Lori anything, especially since she didn't know how she had managed to deliver this to her in the first place. Now that she saw what Lori had gotten for her, her heart was working strangely in her chest. Alice closed the box and took a breath, falling back into the Case family Christmas morning as best she could.

Once the gifts had all been unwrapped, Alice retreated back to her room and closed the door behind her before she pulled out the card from under her pillow. She had gotten many things, but this was the first sign she had gotten from Lori in almost two years. A box of handmade jewelry and a card for Christmas.

The presence of both was more of a relief than Alice realized. It was a sign that she was not only alive, but she remembered her. Between the two, she had no idea if Lori was ever going to come back, but if she had the time to make all of this, then she must be doing all right. She did enjoy making these, even if their parents did not approve and forbade her from ever letting Alice have any of the pieces.

They were beautiful, but Alice couldn't bring these home. It wasn't just that she wasn't allowed them, but she couldn't even talk about Lori at home. Her parents had decided that she did not exist, and Alice wasn't sure if she could ask Ms. Miller without getting her in trouble as well. But this, as vague as it was, was a sign she was okay. It was as good a sign as any.

Alice set the rest of her gifts aside and got ready for the day. Since she was not at home, she decided to wear the earrings, even if they were much too nice for the rest of the comfortable clothes she chose for today. They jingled in her ears as she walked, making her smile with every step. She didn't know what the rest of the day would bring, but she felt better with the knowledge that her sister was with her in some way.

She heard Adrianna in the kitchen and found her helping Ryan and Joe with the vegetables for Christmas dinner. "You didn't do your hair and makeup," Alice noticed, looking at Joe. She'd expected him to be a bit more dressed by now, but he looked like he did at school.

"I'm not going anywhere today," he told her.

"You have been around an awful lot though," Ryan noted. "Usually you and Travis are out constantly during the holidays."

Joe shrugged. "It's been snowing pretty hard this year, and the heater in Kay's garage is busted, so we're just going to pick up again in the summer."

Alice smiled and went closer to Adrianna. "What are they talking about?" she asked quietly.

"Oh! Joe's in a band."

"Come by during the summer and you can see him play." Alice turned around to find Claudia leaning into their conversation. She smiled from Alice to Ryan. "Is there anything I can—"

"No," Ryan said quickly, his smile strained. "It's okay, Claudia. We've got this."

"There must be something I can do to help. You kids can't do all the cooking."

"Please, Claudia," Ryan said, smiling as he spoke. "We do not need another kitchen fire. We are *not* getting delivery on Christmas."

Claudia sighed dramatically, her smile only widening. "If you insist. But if you change your mind…"

Alice's eyes were wide as she watched Claudia leave the kitchen, jaw clenched and staying very still the whole time. Claudia was their mother, wasn't she? You couldn't just talk to one of your parents like that. They were going to get in so much trouble. She didn't know how Adrianna and Joe could both be smiling about it, but it looked like no one else was worried about how much trouble they were going to be in from that.

"Every time she is in this kitchen, she sets something on fire," Ryan said, smiling at Alice. "I don't suppose you know anything about cooking. I could actually use an extra hand with the stuffing."

"I... What do you need me to do?" she asked, forcing herself to not worry about this. They weren't for some reason, instead Ryan quickly setting her to work cutting and mixing the stuffing on the stove and getting it ready to put into the giant turkey they managed to procure for dinner.

"I don't know if dad needed to get one this big this year," Ryan muttered as Alice finished with the stuffing. "We're down two boys and I don't think you're going to make up for them."

"More leftovers," Joe offered, a look of concern flickering over his face. "It's weird that they aren't here, though. Did Lance ever say where they went?"

"It's fine," Adrianna said. "They'll turn up eventually, right?"

"Yeah..."

With her part done, Alice quietly excused herself from the conversation and the kitchen. For a family this close, she felt guilty for not returning Adam and Matt in time for the holidays. At the very least, she could take another look through the mirrors for some sign of them. Maybe she could even chat with someone on the other side and see if there was anyone who could help her find them.

She went up to her room and dragged a chair in front of the mirror. Wonderland showed up in front of her and she leaned in close to get a better look at it as she moved the scene to the forest and the long, winding path. She found herself looking up into the trees from the ground most of the time, though she could occasionally get an angle from a little higher so she could see more of the forest.

There was no sign of them anywhere. She kept looking from different angles, hoping for another sign that they were at least there at some point, but all she could tell was that Wonderland may have actually gotten rain. Maybe they were flying. She never really looked up much while she was in Wonderland, but now that so many of the angles pointed that way, she could see clouds that cast no shadows and no sign of any boys from Lucena Academy anywhere.

This was silly. There needed to be a way to lure them out. If they were hiding from the knight, then they wouldn't be on the path. If they were hiding from anything at all, including Tiger Lily, the Cheshire Cat, or even being sucked into the Mad Hatter's tea party — how both of them managed to avoid it this long was a mystery to her — then they would be staying off the path.

But she did know a way to lure them out if they were there. If they were anywhere near the forest, it should draw them out. At the very least, it was worth a shot. She got up from the chair and leaned over the dresser, pressing her face into the mirror.

She missed the knock at the door, though she felt the

hand grabbing her by the shoulder as her face passed through the mirror. She was pulled back and the words caught in her throat, along with her breath. Wonderland vanished and she was pushed away from the dresser. Her heart hammered in her chest and her mind struggled to come up with a reasonable explanation for what she was doing.

Lance stood between her and the mirror, panic on his face. There were words, but his moving lips made no sound.

"Hi," Alice said, breathing a sigh of relief. Lance knew about Wonderland. She would not need to explain. She was more curious about why he was here at all. She glanced at the door, finding it open. She could have sworn she closed that.

"What were you doing?" he demanded, keeping his voice down.

"Trying to find Adam and Matt," she told him. "I thought I saw one of them a while back and—"

"I thought you weren't going to be doing any of this 'Going into that place' stuff here! You're supposed to be taking time off of nearly getting killed over there, right?"

"I haven't nearly gotten killed over there in a long time," Alice said. "Not since the Queen of Hearts tried to behead me. And even then, the King of Hearts made sure that never actually happened. And the hearts being removed don't really *kill* you, so it's not that bad. Even Tiger Lily wasn't *that* bad. I don't think she was really going to—"

"Who's Tiger Lily?"

Alice stopped talking immediately, looking at him for a long moment before realizing what had happened. Unlike Evan, Lance had not kept his memories of the time she was away. As far as he knew, Alice had not disappeared for a whole month while the school had dealt with investigations trying to figure out where she had gone.

She shouldn't have said anything. Lance looked even more panicked now.

"No one," Alice said quickly once she picked up on what was going on. "Forget about it. And I wasn't going back, I was just going to see if I could call them from here. It's hard just looking when you can't say anything, so I thought maybe if I just, you know, said something they might come out of hiding."

"They won't come out just because you call them," he said. "Just leave it for now. You don't have to keep looking for them while you're here."

"It's hard not to," Alice told him. "You guys don't even realize how much you miss them and it's *my* fault that they're over there. And besides, I can look for them without ever going over. See?"

Alice pointed to the mirror, which showed Wonderland, and then moved to show another part of it. Then another. There were people walking through it, this time Alice making out the Duchess wandering through the foreground holding something in her hands and being led around by a very frustrated chef that added too much pepper to everything out of habit.

"What's she holding?" Lance asked, glancing at the door before peering into the mirror a little closer.

"I think it's her heart," Alice said, feeling the worry well up in her throat. It was moving and beating in her hands. The memory of putting the White King's back in his chest came back with a strange tingling sensation that she didn't know how to process. She knew how to put them back now. Maybe she should go back, just for a moment, even if she felt like ice water was running through her veins…

"So you're not going back there?" Lance asked, bringing her attention back to him.

"No," Alice said. She forced herself to look away from the mirror and let the scene change as it wanted to without her. "Just looking from this side. I'll only go if it's to drag them back. But they're hiding really well and I don't know where else to look without actually going over there. Even when I *am* there, I'm not sure where else they might be."

"Have you tried Neverland?" he asked.

"Where?"

Lance shrugged. "It was a place the Queen of Hearts mentioned. Apparently they still have their hearts and don't love her yet, so she was going to go try and get them all or something. It was all kind of crazy, but everything over there was. I figured it was just another part of Wonderland, you know?"

"Not any part I've ever heard of," Alice said, trying to think of anywhere she hadn't thought of yet. She'd been all over the place, but there were probably parts that she'd never been to. Tiger Lily had come from somewhere that was dead, or whatever it was she had said. It was possible that there was a part of Wonderland called Neverland that she just hadn't been yet. The chess pieces had to come from somewhere, right? "Did she say where it was?"

Lance shrugged. "Beyond the edge of Wonderland? Something like that. It was supposed to be this whole world that was completely undiscovered. They were going to go out and march on it and take all their hearts. Well, probably before the dragon went through and destroyed the castle."

He grinned, but Alice was already deep in thought. There had to be someone who mentioned something about Neverland before. She'd talked to so many people in Wonderland now, but she couldn't think of a single person who ever mentioned the name before. And if Wonderland was good at anything, it would be talking about gossip that no one cared about.

Except she cared about it. Which meant they probably were never going to mention it to her.

Her mind went to Tiger Lily and her heart leapt in her chest. She had a feeling that Tiger Lily would know something about this place. She was so normal, which made her so strange in Wonderland. She might know what this place was and where to find it, but Alice was not ready to see her again. After everything, she was ready to run from her should they ever meet again rather than ask her questions. There had to be something else. Some way to find it without asking her.

"Trying to decide where to hide a land of nevers in a land of wonders?" came a voice from the mirror. The wide purple eyes came into view first, followed by his grin, and then the purple fur of the Cheshire Cat. "Such strange things to think of on such a strange day. Such odd celebrations you have, where you bring the outdoors inside and eat small people after you have baked them."

Lance jumped, keeping himself between Alice and the mirror as he glared at Cat, but Alice only let out a tired sigh. "Hello Cat," she said, already anxious for this to be done with.

Lance faltered in front of her, looking between Cat and Alice. "Cat? Not *that* Cat..."

Cat purred in the mirror, looking back to Lance, but continuing to speak to Alice. "This one again," he said. "I do hope he's calmed his temper since last time. It wouldn't do for a nice girl to be playing with boys who push poor cats through mirrors."

"The hell are you talking about?" Lance asked, his voice small and lost.

"*You* pushed me through a mirror," Alice told Cat firmly. "What do you want?"

The Cheshire Cat paced along the bottom of the mirror. She thought he might be talking to her through a small pond, since there was a distinct cloud in the sky that Alice hadn't ever seen before. Did Wonderland even have clouds? Or, for that matter, rain that would have allowed her to look out into the forest through?

Cat smiled, looking Alice over and taking her in. "You know precisely what I would like, Alice," he said. "Strange things have begun happening. People walking around with their hearts in their hands rather than on their sleeves. Very unseemly either way. I've come to distrust this turn of events and would greatly appreciate any means of leaving that may be spared."

"I'm not letting you out," Alice said. "Why don't you just leave like you did before if you want to get out of there so much?"

"I am curious, Alice dear. Have you added another book to your library? Mine seems to have fallen short."

Alice frowned. She wasn't entirely sure what he was asking, but knew better than to try and get him to tell her. "My library's been a little empty of late," Alice said.

"Empty?" he asked, this time genuinely curious and his grin threatening to widen into a maniacal width. "It cannot be empty. Why, you've barely read it."

"What's he talking about?" Lance asked.

"I got rid of it," Alice said. It was technically true. "I guess you'll never know what drove the Queen crazy now."

"It is a shame and a loss to not know that," he said, sounding more disappointed, though there was a hint of that dangerous madness in his words. "I would have liked to see if it would have driven you the same kind of mad. But that is not the only reason you were meant to take the book, Alice." His eyes were sharp as they stared at her, his tone disapproving.

Alice wasn't sure what had caused this change, but she was caught somewhere between nervous and wanting nothing to do with it. She wanted him to go away, but she had also never seen him looking quite so serious before. It was unsettling. "If you wanted me to do something with it, then you should have told me what you wanted."

"You were to keep the book and keep it from falling into unfortunate and curious paws. Wonderland wanted you to cure it of the harm the books had caused."

"Books?" Alice asked. "There's more than one?"

"Alice, just make him leave," Lance told her.

The Cheshire Cat laughed a humourless, hollow laugh. "If there were only one, then the troubles would be quite small indeed. Alas, for all to have fallen into such disrepair, several holes were made and several books fell and several ideas were laid to seed in the soil of Wonderland. The blossoms have been causing quite the mess, though one let me through before and again when you were not looking. I had hoped you were the one who had taken it from me from where I had hidden it, in a much more clever place than you I might add. A book in the library. It is precisely where it belongs and therefore not a place to hide at all."

"You didn't find it," Alice said. "Not on your own."

"You're not supposed to be here," Adrianna said, appearing through the door and looking in the mirror. "Leave us alone!"

"Oh good, you did keep the pretty one."

"Are you done, Cat?" Alice asked. She wasn't sure why, but she now had two people in her room with the Cheshire Cat in the mirror. She couldn't have more people show up. It was only a matter of time before someone who didn't know came in to see this.

"You would do well to get that book back, Alice," Cat warned her. "Wonderland is not the only land that is falling."

The questions that started to form on Alice's tongue were silenced as the mirror returned to being only a mirror reflecting the room once more. She let out a breath, letting herself relax as she looked back to Adrianna and Lance. They both looked almost angry, though Alice wasn't sure why.

"Hi," Alice said to Adrianna. "Sorry. He still shows up sometimes."

Adrianna looked away from the mirror, though she didn't look happy about it. "I was just coming to get you for dinner," she said. "Lance was supposed to do it, but he didn't come back."

"A little distracted," Lance said. "Who was that?"

"That was the Cheshire Cat," Alice told him. "He's annoying. But dinner smells good." She smiled, the comment very true. With the door open and Alice needing the distraction, she paid attention to the scent of the meal wafting up the stairs and reaching even this far into the house. With any luck, they would take the hint as well.

"I have so many questions," Lance told her. "But after dinner. They'll wonder what's going on soon if we aren't down."

Adrianna smiled and led the way, Alice more than happy to fall back into whatever their Christmas traditions for dinner were. Whatever the Cheshire Cat meant, that could wait until after she was happily full. There was no need to let him ruin what was otherwise the best Christmas she'd ever had.

CHAPTER 5

Back to the Grind

ONCE ALICE GOT through Christmas, the rest of the holiday passed almost calmly. Well, calm compared to the first half of it. There was time for relaxing and doing very little at all, and Alice even managed to get her homework for the break done between just hanging out and listening to Adrianna and her family talk about nothing. Claudia was suddenly overrun with something to do with her work and spent much of the rest of the holiday in her office on the other side of the house, which Alice was perfectly fine with.

The only other thing they really did was New Years. It turned out that they celebrated by staying up until midnight and setting off fireworks in their large back yard while making as much noise as they could manage. It was probably a good thing that their house was somewhat isolated from the rest of the neighbourhood, because Alice was sure there would have been a noise complaint against them. Her father liked to do that on New Year's when people were being too loud.

The flight back to school was a lot easier than the one there. Besides Alice, Evan was the only one anxious to head back to school, especially now that graduation was so close for him. For almost everyone else, there was homework that had been left until the plane.

Between the flight and the taxi from the airport, they arrived at school fairly early in the day, leaving Alice plenty of time to unpack before anyone else showed up. She preferred not to encounter any more people just yet, liking the down time after spending so many hours crammed in a small space with so many people once more. They took turns in the shower to clean the feeling of travel off of them, and didn't realize how long they'd been in the room until they heard a knock on the door.

"Hey guys!" Heather said, letting herself in as soon as they opened the door. "How was the break?"

"Alice came over!" Adrianna told her. "She spent the whole break with us."

"It was a lot of fun," Alice said, trying to find a spot for the jewellery that Lori had given her. She didn't really have a box to put it in, but there was probably space in one of the drawers. She just needed to make sure she didn't break it.

"Must have been," Heather said, smiling and hiding something behind her eyes. "Those are pretty."

Alice smiled and brought the jewelry over to her. "My sister made them."

"They're gorgeous," she said, marvelling at them. "Wait, I thought your sister was missing."

"Not missing, exactly," Alice said, smiling. "She sent these."

"They're nice. Any word on when she's coming back?"

Alice hesitated. "She didn't say."

"Okay, not prying," Heather said, giving back the jewelry. She leaned in closer, glancing at Adrianna. "Hey, have they found Mark or Matt yet?" she asked, much more quietly.

Alice shook her head. "They don't really talk about it much, though," Alice said, which was the truth. They didn't, though she caught glimmers of deeper concern there than any of the Cases realized they had about their missing siblings. "Just don't mention it."

Heather nodded, looking concerned herself about it. She had a bit of a thing for Matt. Alice thought she might actually be able to tell him apart from the his brothers if she had to.

"How about you?" Alice asked.

"You know," Heather said, shrugging. "Family. Television. The usual stuff."

"Everyone else must be almost here by now," Adrianna said. "Do you want to go downstairs and see?"

They headed down to the foyer and met up with Robert and Kevin, both of whom were looking well rested and talking with some of the other boys in their year. It ended up being a much larger conversation than Alice really wanted. Somehow, they ended up drawing in half of their year in a large conversation, with Adrianna heading off to talk to other people and leaving Alice to try and make small talk with her classmates.

They exchanged stories, all with different tales of this awesome thing they did or that great thing they got. Robert spent some of the holiday working on something for the gaming club, so he was excited to go back and show it off. Kevin spent the time off in Thailand, which he seemed annoyed about. Somehow, he was never permitted to go back to Korea, despite having come from there. Alice thought it was a little weird, but he got to take interesting vacations around the world to see his father, so it couldn't have been that bad. Adrianna was quick to talk about the break for both of them, though would say nothing about Mark or Matt.

When the stories started to turn into a study session for everyone who didn't get their homework done over the break, Alice excused herself back upstairs to her room, leaving

Adrianna downstairs to mingle and enjoy herself. Alice hoped everyone would be so content with hearing about the holidays from Adrianna that they wouldn't even notice that she was gone.

She put her watch back on and she got up on the dresser. With one last look to the closed door, she walked through the mirror into Wonderland.

SHE GREETED WONDERLAND with a call of, "*Ábedecian gamenian snytrian eormencynn hércyme!*" and then hopped up onto the bridge to sit on the stone rail. Her feet dangled over the edge so she could look more easily down into the water. It moved in little circles around the rocks at the bottom, looking so clear and a little too perfect to be real.

Absently, Alice fidgeted with her watch, feeling the bite of the clasp on her wrist. It *was* real, and she could feel herself relax for the first time in a very long time. As much of a pain as Wonderland was, she was glad to be here instead of back in the dorms. After spending the holidays at Adrianna's, she was starting to realize she needed the time away from all those people.

But she also knew that Wonderland would not leave her alone for long. She was not surprised when her reflection in the stream showed something purple fade into existence beside her. She felt the warm body covered in fur draped over her shoulder a moment later and Cat's eyes stared down into the water to meet her own. "You have the dullest of hobbies, Alice."

"Hello Cat," she said. There was no getting rid of the Cheshire Cat if he wanted to follow her, but at least now he seemed harmless. There was no mischief in his voice, only a sense of dejection as he gazed down into the water to watch her.

"Wonderland has chosen poorly again," he said. "You are much less clever than the last one."

"You're mad I gave away the book before it drove me mad."

"We would be so lucky if you became mad," he said. "If you have already chosen your loyalties, then you could at least let me choose mine. Though I suppose there is still a way out for me as well. You have not taken away all my ways out, even if you think you are clever."

"Then stop bugging me to let you out and leave me alone," Alice said. "I had to do it. If I didn't, I'd already be gone forever."

She didn't speak as harshly as she could have, finding herself very curious. The Cheshire Cat was speaking almost plainly, though what he was talking about still eluded her. A part of her wanted to find out what it was, while another wanted nothing more to do with whatever he thought she was meant to be here for. She had no desire to hear how buying herself another year was a bad decision.

She tore her eyes up from the water. The forest around her remained quiet and distinctly devoid of any sign of Adrianna's brothers. That, she reminded herself, was why she was here, and not to listen to whatever Cat had to say.

"Tiger Lily would like to see you again."

"I don't want to ever see her again," Alice said, looking down at her watch. She'd waited nearly long enough already. She should move, but she didn't know if Cat would follow. "I just need to not get caught again."

"You think it so simple," he said.

"She wouldn't have caught me last time if I knew it was her. I know better now. Adam and Matt won't hide from me like she did."

"So sure of yourself," he said, the amusement in his tone sounding a lot more like his usual self. Alice frowned, sure this meant he would go back to telling her nothing. "She is better than you are in so many ways. Much quieter. Even less polite."

"I'll be fine," she told him, though now she found herself looking more carefully at the trees around her. She could already feel eyes on her and no one coming out into the open to claim them. The memory of Tiger Lily taking her down with a dart came back to mind, and how helpless she had been to stop her.

"The mouse always thinks it will do well when it tries to steal cheese from the cat."

"I'm not a mouse," Alice said. Those eyes were boring into the back of her skull and they felt like they were getting closer with every moment.

"Perhaps you are the cheese, then," Cat said, grinning and stepping over her, his tail brushing up against her face as he affectionately nuzzled the top of his head against her arm. It was like he was trying to keep her here and she did not want any part of it.

There was a crack in the trees above them and Alice jumped off the bridge, landing in the ruins of the Duchess' castle. She looked around and that feeling of eyes were gone, but the Cheshire Cat was next to her a moment later. With a sigh, she turned to the rest of Wonderland and yelled, "*Ábedecian gamenian snytrian eormencynn hércyme!*" before taking a seat amidst the rubble.

"Scared so easily," the Cheshire Cat teased her.

She ignored him and looked at the destruction around her. The walls and foundation of the castle were still here in bits and pieces, though she didn't know how sturdy it was now that the roof had fallen on it. There were bits of wall still standing and parts of the furniture were intact. She had no idea how they managed to destroy the place, really, besides possibly blowing it apart from the roof and letting it crumble down to crush everything below.

"Better to be careful than to get my tongue stolen by an opportunistic cat," Alice told him. "How long are you planning on keeping me company today?"

"Why, until well after you go," he said.

"You aren't coming through with me," Alice told him, still looking around at the ruins. She stepped away from him to look at the remains of a nicely upholstered chair, then to another area with a tapestry that had fallen, then another section that still had most of a statue. The statue didn't look quite right, though. There wasn't a real shape to it, more like the abstract art they saw in their textbooks sometimes rather than an actual piece that she would expect in Wonderland.

Not that she didn't know better than to expect anything from Wonderland.

"Perhaps not," he conceded, continuing to follow along after her with only his head while his body basked in the sun.

"You have another way out," she said. "That's what you said."

"I have said a great many things," he told her. "Foolish girl you are if you believe every word from a cat. But perhaps you will help me and finally rid me of that way out."

"No." Alice didn't even look at him or listen to any of his

words beyond the request for help. "You have given up any help I might have offered you when you threatened me with that book. Oh, and when you trapped me in Wonderland. And covered up all the mirrors so I couldn't find them. Let's not forget that one. You're lucky I'm even talking to you."

"Ah, but this is a matter of importance to the guardian that Wonderland has chosen to stand for herself," the Cheshire Cat insisted. "You would do well to listen to me, Alice. I know far more of the events unfolding than you could hope to as you hide in that school of yours. Though you have been trying very hard to forfeit that title, Wonderland continues to insist."

"Guardian?" Alice asked, the word catching her interest. "The Bandersnatch keeps calling me a hero, you say guardian, and I don't remember agreeing to anything."

"Heroes are often thrust into their paths without their knowledge and never realize it until well after their task is complete. Your task is much simpler, Alice. Much to my disappointment, you have been figuring it out all on your own. A clever little piece of cheese you are."

"You mean keeping you from getting out of Wonderland?" Alice asked. It was the only thing that he might acknowledge she did without knowing in the least how she did it. "If all I have to do is keep you from getting out of here, then that's a pretty easy job. I can do that."

The Cheshire Cat let out a humourless laugh, his grin growing wide and his eyes wider as he stared at Alice, looking crazier than ever. "Simplicity is not becoming of your task. You are not only the door to the kitchen that will keep the mice from catching the cheese, but also the traps inside to rid the cheese of the rats that have already found their way inside. You keep Wonderland from letting any of these rats in, but you have yet to get rid of the rats that have snuck in. We left the door open for too long while you were away."

Alice tried to follow and puzzle it out, but the metaphor was almost too straightforward, at least in part. She was meant to keep things that did not belong out. But also to get rid of the things that did not belong out of the kitchen that was Wonderland as well? She didn't know what that meant. She didn't know what the rats were and there were already plenty of things that were in Wonderland that didn't belong.

Like the Jabberwocky. And Tiger Lily. And the brown book.

"I need to get rid of the Jabberwocky again?" Alice asked. "Where else am I supposed to put him? I don't even have the book to trap him anymore!"

"There are so many mice in the kitchen that I'm sure that particular one can wait," Cat said, floating backwards easily, the rest of his body coming to join his head now that she was in a sunnier spot. "And you are not a very good door at all. Not that any of the doors before were terribly good at being doors, either. Wonderland is very bad about doors, but decent about their dormice."

"Just speak plainly," Alice said. He was obviously trying to tell her something, but she had no idea what doors had to do with anything. He didn't know how to speak normally, she realized, but that was no reason to speak like a lunatic.

"I have no way out of this place now," he said. "You sit in the ruins of my last prospect."

Alice turned the words over in her mind, remembering something Cat mentioned at Adrianna's house. "Did you have one of the books?" she asked. "Another book like the brown one? Did you keep it?"

"As observant as ever, aren't you?" he asked, smiling. "I have seen the madness that the books cause, so I found the book again and found another soul to do what was needed. We used to have forest up to the border of Wonderland, you know. It's been replaced with grass and people now."

"You hid the book, didn't you?" she asked. "You hid the book where no one would find it in case I sent you back again."

"Of course," he said. His eyes were sparkling as he watched her, glee dancing in the violet hues. "So lucky that I was able to come back at all, really. I had been trying to get the mirror to open for me once more, and then it did. Just like that! I thought perhaps I finally did something right, but it seems our dear Guardian has been making deals with interesting creatures who do not know what balances they tip."

Alice didn't much like being reminded that she had to keep making those deals. She had gotten in enough trouble already and she was going to pay the price for it very soon. She needed to get Adam and Matt out of Wonderland before that happened so they wouldn't be trapped here. She didn't have any idea how she was going to get the Bandersnatch back into Wonderland, so she needed to focus on doing everything else she could so that no one else would pay for her mistakes.

"So where did you hide this book?" Alice asked. "If I'm supposed to be getting all the mice out of the kitchen or however this is going, I'm going to need that book too, right?"

"It has been hidden away so securely that I no longer know where it is."

"You lost it?" Alice was shocked and she didn't know what she was going to do with that information.

Cat shrugged, not knowing what else he could do besides continue to float there. "I suppose I could hardly expect a book that is so exquisite at moving other people to stay in one place itself. I thought perhaps it had found you, though it seems it knows what you do with precious and dangerous reading."

Alice resisted the guilt welling up in her. No, this was not something she was going to worry about right now. First, she needed to get the boys out of Wonderland. Then, if she could think of something, she would come up with a way to beat the Bandersnatch's bet. And after that, only if she could manage to get everything else done, then she would worry about all this stuff about mice in the kitchen and finding books that needed safekeeping and whatever else he was talking about. This was really all a little too much.

"You might also want to touch the frosting back up on the cake that the mice have already gotten to," Cat added, looking off into the rubble as something came up out of it. Alice looked as he vanished.

Coming towards her was a fox, the one she had seen crossing the bridge a long time ago, holding his heart. He didn't seem to know where he was going or what he was doing, just that he should continue to walk with his heart in his hands, still beating and thankfully not bleeding.

Alice watched from a distance, looking for anyone following him. There might be cards looking to drag an escaped member of the kitchens back, or maybe they were using him to lure out his friends from hiding to get captured.

The fox continued to wander along the path, not really looking at anything at all. There wasn't anywhere to hide, though there was a bog a little further on that cards would not do well in. There were creatures that lived there, but she had already seen that the bog had been largely ransacked and she didn't encounter many that stayed in their houses after that.

It was kind of sad to watch him. She didn't know how else to describe the sight of a fox in a waistcoat wandering with his heart in his hands. She should help him, she knew, though she didn't want to get involved in any more of Wonderland's dealings. But she was the only one who knew how to help him. After all that pain from last semester, some good could come of it.

Alice walked out of the rubble and appeared before the fox, her chest tight as she decided what she would do. He stopped, looking up at her with dead eyes, and did not move. He just watched her in a way that was unsettling, like he wasn't even there, and his heart beat in his hands with a very steady rhythm that she was too familiar with. She tried not to think of the room of hearts or the box on the desk, but cold fear thrummed through her with every beat.

"Hello," she said to the fox. Her nerves needed to settle, though his dead eyes staring at her did not help. She looked down at the heart, but her attention went to his hands. Since when did foxes have hands? Then again, the Hare had hands, as did the White Rabbit. This was all very off topic. She needed to focus or she would never do this. "Did you want me to put that back for you?"

The fox did not react. She didn't expect him to. "Just stay

there, okay?" she said. She'd done this before. She had nearly collapsed with the effort of doing this. The words, the movements, and the actions were burned into her memory more so than anything else that happened the rest of the month. But she had done this before and she would do it again.

She held out her hand and moved it in a small circle. Her mouth moved to say the words that she could almost read from her memory, but they eluded her conscious mind. She stopped thinking and let them fall out of her mouth instead as the heart caught on her hands. Her mind went to the image that came up. The Fox, thankfully, was holding his own heart. He did not resist as it lifted out of his hands.

The next words flowed out of her as well like they were second nature and she moved her hands in a wide ring around her. The heart flung itself off the ring and flew into the Fox. She saw the recognition start to come up on the Fox's face, looking shocked and disturbed for a moment that something had just plunged back into his chest against his will.

Alice twitched her wrist, remembering how the heart was meant to be aligned. She felt it snap back into place, reconnecting to everything that it was meant to connect to. Alice let her hand drop as the fox fell to his knees.

He blinked after a moment, and then brought a hand to his chest. "My word," he said, looking around. His eyes eventually fell on Alice.

"Hello," she said, offering a small curtsy. She found herself exhausted from the effort, but she was not going to give him any reason to tell her that she was rude. "My name is Alice. I do hope that it is all right that I returned your heart to you."

"How did I get here?" he asked instead, looking around. "Why, I had an audience with the Queen! She was quite perturbed that I had a bit of a taste for her eggs, you see. Perhaps if she made sure the hens laid less tasty eggs, then she would not have such a predicament. But there was a moment where she seemed so enraged…"

His mind wandered and he tapped his heart. "You put my heart *back* you say?" he asked, slowly coming to realize what happened to him. "Why, my girl, my Alice. That is a very kind thing for you to do for a stranger for no compensation! And you won't be getting any compensation from me, mind. We did not agree to any terms."

"I wouldn't dream of it," Alice assured him. "Nor will I ask."

"Then you have my thanks." He grinned. "I shall do you the honour of telling everyone about your lovely services, of course. For doing such a wonderful job. It feels just right in there."

Alice smiled and immediately felt like there were eyes following her. Not bad eyes, just curious ones that started to emerge from the bog. Small animals and people who all looked to her like she was something much more than she really was crept closer.

"Did you see that?" they whispered to one another. "She put it back!"

"Can she do that with everyone?"

"Can she make my mummy come back?"

"What will she ask? It is never free, a thing like that. She looks like a greedy thing."

Alice should have known this was a horrible idea. She was gathering a crowd and already she wanted to run.

The Fox had something more to say on the matter and turned to address them. "Ladies and gentlemen," he said, sounding much grander than Alice hoped he would. "I present to you my wonderful young protégé, the dear Alice, who can return all your hearts to your loved ones. All that you need do is make a small donation to myself and Alice will—"

"To you?" Alice asked.

"But of course," the Fox said. "I am your manager. I have discovered you and you will owe me for that."

Alice gave the Fox one last look and turned away to find a mirror back to her dorm. She could feel her head starting to ache and she wanted nothing more than to get some rest before classes began in the morning.

CHAPTER 6

For a Friend

LIFE AT LUCENA Academy very quickly settled into the very familiar routine of last semester. Alice was being careful about not getting stuck in Wonderland by returning early every night as soon as she felt those eyes starting to follow her everywhere she went. Alice worried that those eyes might be the Case brothers, but they couldn't move that fast and they surely weren't thinking daggers into her skull just for trying to rescue them. A dull ache in her mind continued to linger, but she ignored it as she sank back into her studies.

The only oddness that Alice noticed was that Adrianna was less interested in hanging out with them lately. She started studying with one of the boys from their class named Wyatt, who kept her busy by trying to help her out with her math. Kevin watched them carefully, but he made no move to stop it, instead keeping to his own homework, muttering something about how it's easier now that she's only got one brother in middle school to keep an eye out for her. A grin crossed his face.

Alice didn't really know what any of that meant until later that week. She took the evenings after homework and before her foray into Wonderland to write in her new notebook that Adrianna had gotten her for Christmas. Her current project wasn't recording her adventures, but trying to make sense of the images of the brown book that Evan had sent her. While she could still remember enough to piece together what was on the pages, her memory of the time was hazy and starting to fade.

Adrianna fidgeted from her bed, blushing and looking a little embarrassed. "Hey Alice?" she asked, drawing her attention. "What do you think of Wyatt?"

"He seems nice," Alice said, not sure what she was getting at. "You've been spending a lot of time with him, though. You'd know better than me."

"I think I like him," she said. She said it in a way that was a little different from what Alice was used to. She knew what liking someone normally was and you didn't say it with that slightly wistful and dreamy air to it. She'd never heard the tone outside of the movies she'd seen, and from Sarah when she was still here and playing matchmaker.

"Like him?" Alice asked.

"Yeah," she said. "He wants me to get dinner with him. Like, the two of us maybe."

"That's great!" Alice was pretty sure this was a good thing. It sounded like she had a date, and people were usually pretty happy about those. "When?"

"On Saturday," she said. "But he promised he'd do something with Nike before he asked me and he doesn't want to cancel on him, so now he's trying to find someone to go with him too. Which is good! I don't really know what to do on my own like that, so more people would be nice."

Alice looked up from her notes and turned back around, seeing Adrianna as she kept playing with her fingers. It was easy to see how nervous she was and Alice wasn't sure what she was supposed to do.

She knew of Nike more than she had actually met him. He was also in their year, though she couldn't remember much about him besides a vague image of a loud, sandy blonde sitting behind Adrianna in English. She knew his name was actually Nikolai, but he insisted on being called Nike instead and that was where her knowledge of him stopped.

But finding someone for Nike seemed to be what Adrianna needed so that she could go out with Wyatt. "Have you tried asking Heather?" Alice offered.

Adrianna brightened up a little at that, though her hands continued to play with themselves. "You think she would?"

she asked. "She still seems kinda upset that Matt's not around anymore."

"You can always ask." Alice smiled encouragingly. "I mean, if Wyatt can't find someone else, right? He'll probably find someone."

"Yeah. He'll probably find someone. Are you going back into Wonderland again?"

Alice looked from her notes to the mirror. How casual Adrianna was about her missing brothers always threw her off. Alice needed to get them back, but she was running into nothing but dead-ends whenever she went. "Not tonight," she said. "Tell me about Wyatt instead."

Adrianna sat a little straighter at that, her hands coming apart and falling next to her on the bed. Alice closed the notebook and laptop, settling in to hear from Adrianna what she liked about him. This was what you were supposed to do when your friends liked someone, right? Talk about the boys they liked. She could go back to searching tomorrow.

ALICE WONDERED IF she had done the wrong thing by letting Adrianna tell her about the boy she liked. They talked well into the night and, while Alice liked listening to Adrianna talk about how much she liked him and how she hoped he liked her back, she had no idea what she was supposed to do with this information. It was made worse by the fact that Adrianna kept wandering off with him after class to talk more.

"So are they going out yet?" Robert asked as they walked down to lunch, watching as Adrianna and Wyatt wandered off down the halls.

"Might as well be," Kevin said. "All formalities now, right? I hear something's happening Saturday."

"He wants to take her out," Alice told them. Word of it had already gotten around, and Adrianna was willing to talk about it, so Alice saw no reason not to confirm it. "Apparently he's just looking for someone to go with Nike too."

A look crossed Kevin's face as he looked at her. His eyes went back to Robert's, the two of them talking in looks that Alice couldn't read.

"I'm sure he'll find someone," Alice said. "I mean, I think he likes her too, right? So it'll work out."

"*Someone*," Robert said. Both of them laughed.

The hand on her shoulder made her stop. "Alice, wait up." She knew the voice before she saw Lance — Mike? They were back at school, so it was Mike now — behind her. "You got a minute?" He cast a look at Robert and Kevin next to her.

"We'll meet you in the cafeteria," Kevin said, pulling Robert along.

"Hi," Alice said. She let Mike led her off to the side of the hall, away from the crowds and just out of sight as the rest of the people emptied out of it. He looked concerned, his eyes darting around like he was waiting for something. "Everything okay?"

"Fine," he said. He seemed content by the state of their surroundings, though stayed close and kept his voice low. "Look, I need to know what happened at Christmas. It's seriously been driving me nuts."

"Christmas?"

"*Cat*," he hissed, looking around again before he locked eyes with her. "What the hell was he talking about? I never pushed him through a mirror and it sounds like a lot more happened."

"I don't know what you've been doing with him. Cat's been really weird lately."

"Did something happen last year? Like, right before the break?"

"Nothing important," Alice told him, not looking away.

"Nothing important isn't *nothing*, Alice," he said. Alice could see a bit of madness in his eyes as he spoke and she shrank away from it. She wondered if perhaps Wonderland had left more of a mark on him than she realized. "Something happened. Evan's not telling me."

"He's probably just busy with school. He's in his last

semester, right? He wants to do well so he gets into a good college. Whatever you're worried about is probably nothing."

"It's obviously not nothing," he snapped at her. "I don't know what's going on with Addie lately, but she's never where I think she is to ask her. So that leaves you. And it's got something to do with you, doesn't it?"

Alice had no intention of worrying him by telling him the truth, and she saw her way out. With a look of surprise carefully pasted on her face, she said, "Oh, she's been hanging out with Wyatt."

"Wyatt?"

"One of the boys in our class."

The look on Mike's face changed at that, brows furrowed and frowning. "Are they doing anything *other* than hanging out?"

Alice shrugged. "Not yet. They were talking about maybe going out for dinner or something, but only if Wyatt can find someone for his roommate to go with as well."

"And he hasn't found anyone yet?" A mischievous grin spread wide across his face as he leaned in closer to her. She was getting a very distinct feeling from him, like the Cheshire Cat when he wanted her to do something. "There can't be that many taken girls in your year. What about Heather?"

"She's busy," Alice said, already preparing to say no to whatever it was he was going to ask. "He'll find someone."

"How much do you know about this guy?" he asked. "He an asshole? Anything that I should know about?"

Alice shrugged. "He seems nice enough. Adrianna likes him."

"Addie likes everyone," he told her. "She makes friends with everyone. And she stays friends with them, even if they happen to lose her brothers in a dangerous parallel universe."

Alice felt the guilt hit her like a truck as she looked up at him. She'd been *trying* to get them back. He knew she'd been trying. He even stopped her from trying. The fact was that she'd still lost them to the other side and she wasn't making any progress getting them back. She had gotten very lucky getting Mike back as it was, though as the days wore on, it seemed like she was never going to be able to find the others. And now it seemed he was calling in a favour for her failure.

"You could always double with her," Mike suggested, pulling back and giving her some space to breathe. "I wouldn't ask normally, but I don't know this guy and this is Addie. She's not always the best judge of people anymore."

Alice eyed him at that. "Anymore?"

"It's…" A look crossed his face. It was the same look that crossed all of their faces when they started to get too worried about Adam and Matt being missing. "It's not important," he said finally. "Look, she's very easy to take advantage of and I don't want some asshole giving her a bad time. So I'm asking you to go with her. Keep an eye on her. Take the free meal."

"I don't know what to do on a date," Alice told him. "I'm not going to be any good at this."

"You're a girl. You just have to sit there and look pretty. Just do this for me, Alice. Addie will listen to you if anything does happen."

Alice looked at him for a long moment before she let out a breath. "Fine," she said. It meant no looking for Adam and Matt this weekend, but she would do it if she had to.

CHAPTER 7

Double Date

SATURDAY CAME A lot sooner than Alice thought it would. Though Adrianna and Wyatt continued to spend time together, Alice made no effort to better get to know Nike, nor did he do the same for her. He seemed nice enough from the distance, but Alice was still unsure about all of this. Something about realizing she'd been blackmailed into it was making the whole situation sit wrong.

Even Heather was a lot more excited about it than Alice was. Alice tried, sure, but she didn't really know what you were supposed to do on a date and why she'd be going on one with someone who she had barely met. Which, really, was more her fault than his, but she still wasn't sure quite what she was supposed to do with Heather and Adrianna asking if she was excited.

Alice opted to spend more time in her room deciphering what she could of the brown book until the weekend. It didn't take long for her to get exhausted pretending she was as excited about it as Adrianna. When Saturday rolled around and Adrianna started to go through her closet to prepare for the evening, Alice vanished for a walk and ended up at what was quickly becoming her stable escape spot in the school, sitting in that windowsill by the rooftop garden above the theatre.

She used the time to write and think about anything else. There was a reason she had been roped into this, after all, and she would like that not to happen again. Unfortunately, she still had no leads since that one time seeing one of the brothers in Wonderland. And she didn't have long before she might be gone completely.

It was strange, she knew, that she had accepted that she was going to be gone in a little over a year. There was only one person who might notice she was even gone if she didn't figure out how to get rid of the Bandersnatch. She wouldn't be missed. As it was, her parents sometimes forgot her. Lori wouldn't have to worry about her anymore, though Alice wasn't sure she was worrying about her now. Adrianna had already shown that she could befriend Heather when Alice couldn't relate to her, so she would be fine. Evan might remember her after this was all over, but he would certainly not miss her.

But she couldn't leave them over there. If she didn't find Adrianna's brothers soon, Alice was going to need to focus on the Bandersnatch just to buy herself a little more time. She needed to get them out. It was her fault that they were in there in the first place.

They should have been kicked out on their own, now that she thought about it. When she was in there the first time, Wonderland got rid of her as soon as the Queen of Hearts ordered her dead and she was covered with fully armed playing cards. It had been a year now and only one of the three managed to make it out. She had to bring Mike back herself on top of that, rather than him getting ejected on his own. Shouldn't Wonderland have let them go by now?

Regardless, she needed to figure out something. She could barely get through a conversation with anyone in Wonderland without being called rude, so she didn't know how she was going to talk the Bandersnatch into leaving the solitude of the forest. She could try setting the forest on fire, but she didn't know how she'd even go about doing that. Plus, if the Bandersnatch could make people forget things and put memories into their minds, was he really going to move for something like a fire?

"Shouldn't you be getting ready for your date?"

Alice looked up from her book and writing, seeing Kevin staring at her and walking around to see what she was writing.

She closed the book and clicked the lock shut. Not taking her eyes off him, she sat up and hopped out of the window with the book held carefully behind her. Kevin paid more attention and he would notice if it were suddenly gone.

"What are you doing here?"

"Rehearsals," Kevin said, looking at her oddly. "You must have heard them."

"I wasn't really paying attention," she said. "Sorry." She wasn't aware of any of the rest of the world while she was sitting there. She needed to pay more attention to her surroundings if she was going to be writing about Wonderland in a place without a lock on it.

"I'm surprised you're out at all," he said. "I figured you and Adrianna would be holed up in your room all day picking outfits."

"Heather already picked mine last night," Alice said.

"You sound excited."

Alice could tell he was being sarcastic. She let out an embarrassed laugh. "He seems nice at least." She held the smile for a moment before she let her shoulders drop. "Adrianna needed someone else to go, so I did. I don't even know what you're supposed to do on a date."

"You'll be fine," Kevin told her, sitting on the windowsill and watching her. "And it's just one date, right? If nothing else, you're going to get a free meal out of it."

"I get a free meal every day," Alice told him. "That's what tuition is for."

"Then maybe you make a new friend. Or maybe you end up liking the guy. Or maybe at the end, you go your separate ways and that's it."

Alice shrugged. "Maybe," she said. She hoped Adrianna and Mike would be fine with her just doing this one time. "I don't really know why everyone thinks it's going to be this big thing, though. Adrianna actually *likes* Wyatt, but I barely even know Nike. I just hope I don't embarrass her or anything."

"You'll be fine," Kevin said. "But you should probably be more excited. Usually girls obsess over that stuff."

Alice shrugged. Maybe she should pretend to be more into it than she was. It was a little late now, though, and she just couldn't bring herself to lie to Kevin, not after she explained herself this much. She would have to be a lot more careful next time.

"Do you know what I'm supposed to do?" she asked instead. He seemed to have a lot more answers than she did about all of this and he might be able to give her a little guidance.

He looked a little taken aback by the question, though he tried to recover. "You just kind of talk," he said, though it sounded like he was scrambling. "It's like hanging out with friends but you touch more and kiss sometimes and stuff. But not the first date," he said quickly, though Alice was not sure why. "Like, maybe if it's a really good first date at the end, but I don't think girls are supposed to let the guy kiss them on the first date."

Alice didn't really think it would get as far as kissing. She would really prefer it if it didn't. She didn't know how to do that either. The whole idea of it was weird to her. She definitely didn't want to do that tonight. She would much rather face the Bandersnatch tonight than kiss anyone.

"Anything else?" she asked, almost a little afraid to get an answer. This was like learning Wonderland's rules of etiquette with how strange it all sounded. She didn't understand it, but at the very least, she didn't want to embarrass Adrianna.

"Nike likes to think he's funny," Kevin added. "Even if he's not, just laugh at his jokes. If you don't, he might get offended and you really don't want to make him offended or anything. But, you know, don't fake it too much if it's not funny or else he'll know you're faking it. Just be really subtle and make sure he thinks you think he's funny. Don't be creepy about it, just be natural."

"This is really weird," Alice told him, trying to take all of that in. "Are you sure I have to do all of this?"

"Positive," Kevin said. "But first you have to spend, like, a whole day picking the best thing to wear that you think he'd like to see you in. My sister always went out shopping right before she had a date to find an outfit just for it."

Alice let out a sigh. "I guess I better get going, then. Thanks."

She left, feeling even more stressed about the evening than she was about not being able to find Adrianna's brothers. She really hoped that this wouldn't go too late and she wouldn't be too tired afterwards, since she still needed to go looking for them once they got back. The prospect of running off to Wonderland when they were done was comforting.

In a few steps, Alice was at the doors of the dorm and walking through it to their room. Adrianna was still going through her closet, trying to figure out what to wear for tonight, but Alice was ready to be supportive and at least pretend that she was as interested in all of this as Adrianna was. Whatever she needed to make this night go by quickly.

Apparently, once Alice was there it was easy to figure out what to wear. Where Heather had apparently asked a lot of questions, Alice was direct in saying what would and would not look good together based on her limited understanding of fashion. They spent the rest of the hour just putting the clothes hurricane that had exploded in their room away.

"I'm nervous already," Adrianna said, though she was still smiling. "I hope he doesn't think I'm boring."

"You've been hanging out with him all month," Alice

told her, trying to assure her as best she could. She tried to remember how this went in movies. "I'm sure he already thinks you're *fascinating*, otherwise he wouldn't have asked you in the first place."

"You think so?"

Alice smiled at her. She was sympathetic, but she didn't understand what she was so worried about. It was just a boy. Adrianna didn't have any trouble around Kevin or Robert. She had seven brothers. Boys should be absolutely no problem for her, and yet she was nervous.

With Adrianna figured out, Alice put on the outfit of partially borrowed clothes from Heather. It went well with the necklace and earrings that Lori had made for her, complementing the small blue gemstones. If nothing else good came out of the night, at least she got to wear some of Lori's jewellery.

"You two look great," Heather said, immediately getting to work on Adrianna's makeup for the evening. Adrianna didn't have a handle on how it worked yet, and Heather was only helping in applying it for her. "You have to make it look soft and natural," Heather said. "You can't look like you're trying too hard on the first date, you know? You look good, but not like you were *trying* to look good."

Alice knew she was going to forget some of these dating rules by the end of the night. Laugh when it's not funny, but don't laugh too hard. Look pretty, but don't look like you're trying to look pretty. Don't kiss on the first date. There was probably going to be touching. She feared what else was going to come up and so she stayed quiet and let Heather talk, since she seemed ready to spout all the advice she could.

"Just remember, guys love talking about themselves," Heather told them as Adrianna once more voiced her worries that Wyatt wouldn't like her after this. "Just keep asking them about them and they'll keep talking. They like to know how awesome they are, so when in doubt, find a way to say that. You can tell them they aren't awesome after you've gone out with them a few times, but this is a first impression. You have to really sell it. And don't talk about school. We're here all day, so no one wants to talk about it anymore. Ask about what they're interested in and if they joined any clubs or something."

Adrianna seemed to be soaking all this in, but Alice thought this was going to make for a really dull evening. It was nice to get to know other people, but if all they talked about was themselves, it was going to get pretty boring really fast. But, she reminded herself, it was only for one evening.

"Oh, and if he tries to kiss you—"

"Don't let him?" Alice chimed in. She remembered that much from Kevin.

Heather clicked her tongue and shook her head, smiling

all the while. "Alice, we aren't in the dark ages. If you want to kiss him on the first date, you can. But only if you think he's really earned it. I mean, he's not going to try unless he thinks you earned it too, so it all works out. But you have to let *him* do it. I don't care how much you want to kiss him, guys hate it when you try to kiss them first, so you let him start."

Alice had no plans of letting Nike kiss her at this point. She just hoped that it wouldn't be too long. All these rules were getting silly and she didn't know how she was supposed to keep track of any of them. They all seemed crazy to her and more complicated than figuring out etiquette in Wonderland. Adrianna already liked Wyatt. Wyatt liked Adrianna. Why did she need to be there for a date with his friend?

The advice continued right up until there was a knock at their door at six. Heather was the one who got it, telling them to wait a minute before closing it again. Alice got her purse and coat on while Heather explained that it was always good to make them wait a little before heading out. Alice considered forgetting all of these rules and instead just try to not fall over at some point during the night and embarrass Adrianna. She would be polite and as civil as she could manage. And she would do her best to have fun and get to know Nike. Maybe he would be her friend by the end, though if this date ended up being anything like all these rules, she never wanted to do this again.

Adrianna opened the door a minute later, smiling at seeing Wyatt there to meet her. He was dressed nicely, in a collared shirt and dress pants, which didn't look that much different from their uniforms, for their off campus dining this evening. Alice had yet to go off campus, but it seemed there was a small bistro in a complex just a short ways down the street second years were permitted to visit.

"You look amazing," he said, smiling. Adrianna giggled and thanked him, taking his offered arm and coming out the dorm with him, Alice following afterwards. "Alice, I think you've met Nike."

"Hi," Nike said behind Wyatt, shifting a little as he looked at her. "You're pretty too."

"Thanks," Alice said. He was probably as unsure about this whole thing as she was. Misery did love company, and she could at least be nice about it if he was going to share in the experience with her. "You look good too."

He smiled and offered his hand. Alice took it and they started walking down the stairs and out the door, Adrianna and Wyatt setting the pace for them and not saying much. Nike was the one who filled the empty place where the conversation was supposed to go.

"I hear this place is pretty good," he said. "It's where a lot of the high school goes."

"What's it called?" Alice asked. Her father always seemed

to refer to places by their names and, when someone suggested a place, he would always ask for a name.

"The Blue Lagoon," he said. "You aren't allergic to shell-fish are you?"

Alice shook her head.

"Then I guess tonight is just going to be a night of discovery for you."

He smiled like he told a joke and waited for a reaction from Alice. She tried a small laugh, which seemed to placate him. She could tell this was going to be an awkward evening already as he launched into the story of the time his mother found out the hard way that she was allergic to scallops when she was younger in a little more detail than Alice was comfortable with. Apparently, she now kept him away from all seafood just in case he inherited anything. He hadn't, of course. He tried the stuff in the cafeteria already, so he knew that he wasn't allergic. Alice had nothing to worry about.

Alice wished he wasn't holding her hand so tightly. She really wanted to get out of this already. Still, she did her best to laugh where she needed to and she said nothing otherwise, desperately looking to Adrianna for some means of escape.

Adrianna, however, was happy where she was. Arm in arm with Wyatt, they were talking to one another ahead of them about something that she couldn't make out over Nike. Still, she looked happy enough and Alice was going to at least try to go along with all of this so that she could have a good date. She owed that much to her after losing her brothers. Especially if she couldn't get them back before she disappeared.

They arrived to find their reserved table waiting for them and were seated almost immediately. At this point, Nike was telling her another story about himself and an actor he'd met over the summer who used to date his mother. Alice didn't know who the guy was, or if he was even an actor with how often he mentioned records this guy had dropped, but Alice knew she was supposed to be impressed by it. She tried her best to be and he seemed to believe it, but she hoped the conversation would open up to the whole table now. She needed to hear about something other than Nike.

"I hope you girls don't mind seafood," Wyatt said. "I think you said you liked crab before, right?" Adrianna smiled and nodded, which seemed to cheer him up. "Alice?" he asked.

Alice was just glad that he was giving her a chance to say something. "I don't remember the last time I had any," Alice said. She also couldn't remember the last time she went to a restaurant where people sat down like this. Her parents never took her out, and when she was out with Ms. Miller it was usually something fast and really bad for her. She tried not to let on how completely lost she was, but Alice was very certain that this was something she would screw up if she wasn't careful.

"You'll like this place," he said, smiling encouragingly and looking back at Adrianna, then back to Alice, then to Adrianna again. "Order whatever you like."

They brought the menus and Alice started looking it over. She was grateful that she and Adrianna were on one side together, separated from the boys by a table. She kept feeling Nike kicking at her feet and looking at her. She smiled and tucked her feet out of his way. She hid behind her menu as subtly as possible, trying to get Adrianna's attention to ask what any of this was. She had heard of all these animals, but she had no idea what any of them tasted like.

After having successfully hidden behind her menu for the better part of ten minutes, the waitress came by to take their order. Wyatt and Nike went first, and even Adrianna knew what she wanted, but Alice still didn't know what was good. "What do you recommend?" Alice asked as sweetly as she could manage.

"She'll have the house special," Nike told the waitress. Alice looked back at him and he looked like he'd done her a favour. It was going so well for Adrianna so far that she didn't want to do anything to ruin it, so Alice just smiled, nodded, and handed the waitress her menu with everyone else.

"Trust me, the special is always the best thing to get when you can't pick," Nike said.

"Thanks," Alice said. She was starting to get irritated, but made sure she was still polite. He was only trying to help her. She could be mad about everything later, but while she was in the moment, she needed to try and be accommodating. He was helping her and she would remember that.

"No problem," Nike said. "Besides, I think it comes with a salad."

Alice smiled, not at all sure what the salad had to do with anything. It was probably a nice gesture or something. She didn't mind salad. More than that, with the lull in conversation, she had a chance to hear about anything other than Nike.

"So what clubs did you guys join this year?" Alice asked, looking between the two of them. Heather said to always ask about them, so that was what she was going to do. It would be rude to exclude Nike completely, she knew, and she had to keep being polite for Adrianna's sake.

"Track," Wyatt said. "We're both doing relay and distance. Oh, and I'm in choir with Adrianna this year."

"Adrianna mentioned something about that," Alice said, looking over to Adrianna. She blushed, but didn't say anything.

"Oh, she's been talking about you," Nike chimed in, nudging Wyatt as he flushed.

"Not that much," Adrianna said, blushing even brighter.

"Only good things," Alice assured him. Wyatt's eyes were down on the table, just as embarrassed as Adrianna. "There aren't many guys in the choir. I'm kind of surprised you decided to join."

"Yeah, well," he said, looking a little embarrassed but saying little else.

"I'm more surprised you asked out the Goth guy's sister," Nike said. "And Mike's sister. And the rugby star's sister. Really, I'm surprised you got up the nerve to ask her out at all. You have a lot of scary brothers. I wouldn't want to be him right now."

"They aren't that scary," Alice said, turning back to Nike. "They're all actually really nice if you actually talk to them."

"If you go around wearing spikes, you aren't *nice*," Nike told her. "He'll probably grow up to kidnap kids or something."

Wyatt laughed and gave him a smack in the arm like it was all a joke. Alice wasn't so sure, but everyone else seemed to be going along with it and she let them, laughing nervously and looking to Adrianna. She didn't seem to be taking any offense. "But really," Wyatt said after a moment. "Joe's been crazy helpful with helping me in choir. He's a really good teacher."

"He has a band," Adrianna said. "Or he's in one. He's the singer when we're on holidays."

Nike rolled his eyes as the conversation switched to Joe's band and he gave Alice a look like he couldn't believe that they thought Joe was really such a nice guy. Alice smiled, taking a deep breath and preparing for a very long evening. Adrianna needed her for a little longer and Alice would do that. Mike had reminded her just how much she owed Adrianna. It was the least she could do.

Alice couldn't help but think that she could be in Wonderland looking for her brothers instead of here paying penance for losing them in the first place. That knowledge started to fester deep inside her as Nike continued to try to nudge her feet under the table with legs much longer than Alice had anticipated.

The special, as it turned out, came with a chowder, while Nike's order came with a salad. Before she had a chance to pick up her spoon, Nike reached over and switched their plates, smiling again like he was doing her a favour. "Girls like salad more, right?" he asked, already digging into her soup.

Adrianna and Wyatt were too distracted by their own plates to notice and Alice resigned herself to the salad in front of her. The soup looked more appetizing than the plate of leafy greens, but Nike didn't seem the sort to let her have any of it. He barely even looked up from the bowl, so she was going to do her best to enjoy the salad.

At least it turned out to be a nice salad. There were bits of shrimp in it, and now she knew what the little pink things tasted like. That was a nice thing about the evening. She was getting a chance to try new foods. Nike had even stopped kicking her now that the food was here.

"Hey, you know what this tastes like?" Nike asked, smacking Wyatt on the arm to get his attention. "You know that place on the strip? Like, way on the far end of it?"

Alice learned between the salad and the arrival of the main course that Wyatt and Nike lived in the same part of California, and that there were even better restaurants there. She frowned as he talked. Even she knew that you weren't supposed to talk about an even better restaurant in such loud tones while you were at a different one.

Thankfully, Nike didn't want any of her main course, which looked really good. It was a grilled salmon steak on top of rice, smothered in a creamy sauce with a lemon wedge on the side. She knew enough to squeeze that on the fish. There were a few roasted vegetables on the side as well for her to enjoy.

Nike was too busy with his steak covered in lobster to notice her plate and she was able to actually enjoy the rest of her dinner in peace. Well, except for the conversation, because apparently the steak tasted like it was a second class version of something Nike had eaten somewhere else as well, some place that they should all try some time. It was almost disappointing when he remembered that she was there.

"So Alice, how's the fish?" he asked her.

"It's good," Alice said with a smile. It really was. It smelled wonderful and everything tasted just right. She wasn't sure what kind of rice it was, but it was different from anything she'd had before. She never had much seafood at home, but if all seafood was like this, she would have to try more of it from the cafeteria.

Granted, the cafeteria wasn't quite up to the quality of this restaurant, but after hearing about how much better everything was in California, she figured that the cafeteria might spare her from being around Nike.

Alice stayed as quiet as she could for the rest of the evening. Nike never stopped talking about himself, and she kept looking over to Wyatt and Adrianna, hoping they would interrupt. She was getting tired of laughing at his stories, none of which sounded terribly impressive. She had no idea who all of these people he talked about were. She'd heard of the movies and bands, but having never been allowed to watch many shows or movies growing up, she never learned who they were outside of their roles.

But he had apparently met most of Hollywood through his father, the Hollywood scout. He'd been to parties where kids his age weren't allowed and been complimented by celebrities before. He was even in a movie once in a bit part and might have pursued a whole acting career out of it, but his mother insisted that he have an education. The more Alice listened, the more she wanted to leave.

Adrianna and Wyatt were talking on their own side of the table, though, and Alice's attention wandered toward them while Nike kept talking. Wyatt's family lived around Silicon Valley and did something in the area that he wasn't really able to explain, not that he really wanted to.

When the evening seemed like it was about to wind down, Nike ordered them a round of dessert. It was nice of him, but Alice just wanted to go home. He kept looking at her and she was careful not to make too much eye contact. She smiled and laughed where she needed to and, with no clock in the room or on her wrist, she spent her time watching the other people leaving.

At least dessert was mercifully quick and they left soon after. They walked back to the dorms and Nike steered them toward the long way. Alice was screaming on the inside about it, but she still managed to grin and bear it, even when he took hold of her hand. He kept talking, telling her more stories about himself, and she tried to look interested while keeping an eye on Adrianna.

Neither of Adrianna or Wyatt spoke as they walked ahead, both staying close to one another without touching. Adrianna eventually reached for his hand and he took it, the two of them leaning in close and starting to talk once more. At least she was having a good time, and it looked to Alice like she could handle this dating thing without her next time.

When they finally got back to their door, Alice smiled and gently shook herself out of Nike's grasp. He leaned in, but she slipped back and through the door frame, out of reach of the hug he seemed to be trying to get from her. She smiled at him and nodded before placing herself firmly behind the door and she shut it just enough so that Adrianna and Wyatt could have their goodbye without her watching.

"I had fun tonight," Adrianna told him.

"Maybe we'll do it again?"

"Oh, we should definitely do it again," Nike said.

Alice was happy when the door closed. Adrianna turned back to her, face flushed and a brilliant smile spread wide across it. "That was amazing," she said, sitting back on her bed. Her eyes were filled with memories of the evening and she kept looking at the hand Wyatt was holding like it was a precious diamond. "Wasn't that the best?"

"It was great," Alice said, trying to sound as enthusiastic about it as Adrianna was. She didn't want to ruin the mood of the evening for her. Now that she was away from Nike, she let her mind focus on more important things. Alice took off her coat and removed her jewellery, looking at the clock. They made it back before their ten o'clock curfew and no one would miss her in the morning, so she had time to go looking tonight. She wanted to get moving into Wonderland. For some reason, she felt anxious and wanted to try punching the Cheshire Cat in the face.

"I hope he wants to do it again," Adrianna said, slowly taking off her coat and continuing to look dreamily at everything around her. She went to the washroom, still talking and leaving the door open as she stared at her reflection, though not turning on the water or making any move to try and wash her face. "Tonight was just perfect. And Nike was nice, too. Can you believe he knows all those people? It was a good idea to go with a double date. I don't know what I would have done if I was all alone. Oh, if we go again, Alice, you'll come again, right?"

There was no response. When she looked out into the dorm room, Alice was gone along with the watch on her dresser.

CHAPTER 8

Unexpected Rescue

ALICE DECIDED THE plains were a great place to start. She needed to run and be far away from anything. She would risk running into Tiger Lily for the chance to be completely alone and away from any of the inhabitants of Wonderland for just a little while.

As soon as her feet hit the ground, Alice took off in a run. There was something that she'd been holding in all night, a nervous energy that she hadn't had since she had to go see the doctors. After a night of trying to be sweet and pleasant, she was finally away and out in the sunshine, where she could be free of anyone trying to hold her hand or tell her how great they were.

She almost didn't want to look for Adam and Matt today. But that was what she was here for.

"*Ábedecian gamenian snytrian eormencynn hércyme!*" she called into the wind. Reluctantly, she slowed down and found a place to sit by the creek that ran through the plains, just beside a small cake on an inexplicably placed table with a note asking her to eat it.

She could eat it. It would be nice to be bigger than everything and just stomp around.

Nike, she decided, was someone she did not like and did not want to see again. He was frustrating and Alice hadn't had to work so hard to be pleasant in a very long time. She would still have to see him in classes, but after this, she didn't want to have to deal with him so closely again.

At least Adrianna was happy about the night. Alice almost felt bad about running into Wonderland, but unlike her, Alice wanted to forget about the whole thing. She really did owe her for having thrown her brothers into Wonderland and still not getting them out, but she hoped Adrianna and Mike would not ask her to do anything like that again to make up for it. It cut into her chances to try and bring them back.

She picked up a rock and threw it into the creek angrily. There was nothing she could really do about it. At least it was over. After this, surely Adrianna felt like she could go on a date alone with Wyatt. If they went again, Alice would not have to be there to entertain Nike for them.

She let out a deep breath as she picked up another rock.

As much as she didn't enjoy the evening, she had to remind herself that he didn't seem like a terrible person. He was just annoying. Alice could handle annoying. She was the one who kept walking willingly into Wonderland, where the things that belonged here didn't know how to do anything but be incredibly annoying all of the time. And the things that didn't belong here were much more dangerous.

Another book. Her mind jumped to that as the purple cat appeared at the other side of the stream, smiling at her and watching her while saying absolutely nothing.

"Hello Cat," she said.

"This was not always a plain, you know," he told her. He disappeared from the other shore and appeared behind her, his eyes looking up longingly at nothing. "Why, this was a grove of trees once. But what it was once no longer matters. What matters is now. And you."

Alice didn't like the sound of that. She tensed up and shuffled away, the Cat rubbing his body up her arm and perching atop her head.

"I have heard that you have learned to perform miracles," he said, affixing himself to her head like a stubborn hat. He weighed almost nothing, but she still felt uncomfortable with him up there. When she tried to grab him to remove him, he vanished piece by piece, and then came back when her hands were gone. "A selfish thing for you to return to your school when there are so many miracles left for you to still perform here."

"Let me guess," she said, trying to push him off her head to no avail. "You aren't going to let me go back until either I've returned everyone their hearts or I let you come back through with me, right? Get off!" she snapped finally, whipping her head forward.

He flew into the tall grass on the other side of the stream and Alice fixed her hair. She definitely should have changed. Her shoes were all wrong for walking around here and her feet were already starting to hurt from running. She was pretty sure she was going to ruin Heather's shirt if Cat came back and decided to take a swipe at her for it. She'd have to make sure he didn't.

The grass rustled and she let out an exasperated sigh, shoulders dropping and throwing her hands up in the air. "Can't you just leave me alone?" she asked. She turned and tried to think of where to go next.

He came out of the grass from behind her, Alice not seeing as he tackled her face first into the ground. She twisted out of his grasp and he was gone again a moment later, rolling away into the grass.

"You missed!" Alice yelled at him. She got up to her feet, brushing the dirt off of herself and shaking her head. What he was trying to accomplish with that, she didn't know. "Stupid Cat."

He came out of the grass again, only it wasn't a large purple cat. Instead, a very familiar Native American girl dressed in leather jumped out of the grass and landed on Alice, pinning her down to the rocky bank. Alice's eyes flew open and panic gripped her. She did not want to go back to the hut. She didn't want to be trapped again to relive that long month, drugged beyond reason and barely able to keep herself together. She couldn't be gone like that again. She had nothing else to give the Bandersnatch to make people forget she was gone.

"I wish to speak with you," Tiger Lily said.

"I don't want to talk to you!" Alice said, trying to wriggle her way out of her grasp. Tiger Lily held her firm, her fingers digging in and Alice unable to disappear. Not that she didn't try to get away, but Tiger Lily had her pinned down well and she seemed to know just how to keep her from moving.

"You do not understand," she said. This, Alice thought, was why she wanted to go into Combat Club. Not because she wanted to get beaten up by boys who were too unruly for her to go out with, but so that no one could do this to her anymore. "I wish to explain."

Alice went still, not because she was ready to listen, but because there was something in the sky. Moving closer and with his back to the sun was a boy flying at them with dark hair. Alice's heart skipped a beat, hopeful that this was one of Adrianna's brothers finally appearing to come to her rescue.

Tiger Lily didn't notice until the boy smacked into her, knocking her back. Alice rolled over, but Tiger Lily was faster, grabbing Alice by the arm and yanking her up to her knees. Tiger Lily pulled Alice in close and clapped a hand over her mouth. Alice bit her finger, but Tiger Lily did not care, wedging her finger between Alice's teeth and not even grimacing at the pain.

"Peter Pan," Tiger Lily said, looking around, her eyes up and checking the skies for him again. "This is not your hunt. Leave us."

Alice didn't recognize the laughter that followed. It was musical, almost like a bird's, and entirely mocking. He came down to face her, barefoot and wearing a messy patchwork of clothing stitched together by someone still learning to sew. He was too small to be Adam or Matt, his face too thin, and his features too sharp. His skin was dark, like he'd never spent a day indoors. Only his hair was right. Alice was disappointed, but hoped that he could still help her.

"Since when do your people hunt girls?" he asked, looking at Alice and studying her face carefully. He even looked a little like a bird from this close. "She'll look really silly being cooked."

The faith she had in this boy was already diminishing rapidly.

"She is not going to be eaten."

"Then what do you want with...."

Peter trailed off, looking at Alice from the side then stepping backwards, leaning away almost comically before bringing his face next to her again. "Hey, aren't you that disappearing girl?" he asked, suddenly very excited. His feet lifted off of the ground. "You are! I keep seeing you all over the place! Tiger Lily, have you seen what she can do? She looks around and then, *poof!* She's gone again! And last time she was saying all these silly words and took something from a fox and stuck it *inside him!* It was so cool! Well, for a girl."

Alice thought about using him as a distraction while she escaped, but Tiger Lily didn't seem impressed with him either. There was a definite sense that the two of them knew each other for a while, a familiarity with which he told her about all this and how little she seemed to care. Tiger Lily's grip relaxed as she watched him.

"I am aware," Tiger Lily said. "This is not your business, Peter. Leave."

"You're no fun anymore, Tiger Lily," he said, floating up a few feet, then leaning back down to face her. "You should spend less time with that purple cat."

"My people are going hungry," she told him, her voice

fierce, but her grip loosening even more. "We cannot hunt here. There are no crops to farm. We have injured because of her. And we have no time for you and your games."

Peter looked contemplative for a moment. "You know, I don't think I've eaten since I've come here. I wasn't hungry before now, but I am *really* hungry now."

Alice threw herself down and rolled under Peter, her mind scrambling for somewhere else to go. She knew that Tiger Lily would come after her, but so long as she stayed away from the plains, she would be fine. She just had to not be here, but there were too many places that could be.

Before she could come up with a destination, she felt two sets of hands grab her and her feet left the ground. Peter had picked her up by the armpits and started to carry her off, while Tiger Lily caught her by the ankle and didn't let go when she left the ground as well.

"I only wish to speak with you," she called up to Alice. "Nothing more!"

Alice kicked, Tiger Lily losing her grip and falling back down the short distance to the grass. She rolled and Alice lost sight of her as Peter carried her away, hooting and hollering with laughter as they rose higher into the sky.

Looking down as Wonderland passed under her feet, Alice wondered if she could disappear as she fell if Peter dropped her. She probably could, so long as she knew where she was going. She decided on the White Rabbit's house. She could drop right down his chimney. The last time she'd seen him, the Queen had taken his heart, so it wasn't like he would return home to find her inside again.

She also knew better than to drink anything she might find inside this time.

Down below, she saw a pack of wandering cards with a blank face on one side and red on the other wandering the woods. One carried a sack and several creatures were in tow. Alice figured they were rounding up the ones who got their hands on hearts and escaped. While the creatures were docile and following without a word, the sacks pulsed rhythmically.

"So what is this place?" Peter asked above her as they flew.

"It's called Wonderland," Alice told him, trying not to look and feel like she should be doing something. "It wasn't always like this, though. It used to be a lot brighter. There were more flowers and more people. And all of the people were very annoying."

"Then why aren't you happy?" he asked. "If there's less annoying people, then it's better!"

"You wouldn't understand," Alice told him. "It was better before. A lot more annoying, but this is…It's just…"

"Wrong?"

"Yeah."

"I know," he said, his voice getting very sad as he spoke. They dropped in the air as he did, Alice looking warily below them and picking up her feet as they started to graze the tops of the trees.

"Maybe we should sit down somewhere," Alice suggested.

"You *are* heavy," he agreed.

They found the bridge and Peter set her down on it, Alice sitting up on one edge and watching Peter as he perched opposite her. Alice listened to the forest around her, but she didn't hear anything unusual. There were no creatures looking to have their hearts returned to them, though this was the direction the cards and their following were headed. They wouldn't be able to stay here for too long.

"So your name is Peter," she said, trying to get a few things straight and get the introductions out of the way. "I'm Alice. I take it, you know Tiger Lily."

"Yeah," he said. "Tiger Lily is the Princess of the Indians, so you *have* to know her."

Alice paused at that. "Isn't she Native American?"

"Native what?"

"Indians are from India."

"What's an India? Is that the lake that tastes like bubbles?"

Alice stared at him, trying to figure out if he was joking. So far, he seemed sincere, but she didn't know about this Peter Pan that Tiger Lily seemed so fed up with. He couldn't genuinely not know what India was. He looked about her age, though he seemed a lot younger than that. He must know.

"Never mind," she said. "You don't seem like you belong in Wonderland at all. You make too much sense to be from here. Well, sort of. You make a different kind of no sense than the no sense that everyone here makes. Where are you from?"

"You talk funny."

Alice just stared at him for a long minute. He had to be kidding and, after Nike, she didn't have the patience for it. "Where are you from?" she asked again.

"Neverland," he said. "It's a great land filled with adventures and pirates and Indians and even some mermaids, but you can't trust them. Or that's what it used to be like. Something happened and..."

A dark shadow passed over his face and he went very quiet. Alice remembered Tiger Lily said she came from a land of death. Maybe Peter had seen some of it. His first descriptions of Neverland were so bright and excited, like he liked it there once. Like it was his home once. "I can't go back anymore. I have to save everyone. I'm the hero. But I can't go back."

"What happened?" she asked. She wondered if it was at all like what happened here. Peter said nothing, hugging his knees into his chest and his eyes looking off into the very far distance as he tried desperately not to remember the details of whatever had happened in Neverland.

"I'll go back one day," he said. "I'll save everyone. I'm not scared of anything, and no one's better than me. I'll save everyone."

"That's great," Alice said. She felt bad for him, but she had no words to help him right now. Not with that, anyway. "I hope you can get back and save everyone. In the meantime, though, I should probably warn you a little bit about Wonderland."

"Why, what happened here?" he asked, suddenly perking up and his wide eyes tinged with fear as he looked at Alice.

"The Queen of Hearts happened," Alice told him. "It's a really long story, but stay away from her, the cards, and the Red Knight. The Queen of Hearts... she likes to take hearts. That thing you saw me put in the Fox before? That was his heart. She took it out. I don't really know how he got it, but if she takes it out, you might never get it back again."

"She just takes them out?" Peter asked, his eyes wide and his mouth in a smile, like it was a grand adventure.

"With her hand," Alice said, resisting the urge to curl up as she talked. The memory was still fresh in her mind, but she forced herself not to think back to that day and those images. "She puts them in this room where everything is made with glass and puts all of the hearts just behind it. Just stay away from the castle."

"But that sounds like an evil queen that needs to be taken down! And I am just the hero for the job!"

"That's a stupid idea," she said, sighing heavily. "You're going to get caught and she'll tear your heart out too. At least the book is gone, but she's still dangerous."

"Book?" Peter asked. There was fear in him now, that confidence cowering down into that of a small child once more. "A black book?"

"A brown one," Alice said, suspicious as she watched him. "Is there a book in Neverland?"

"What happened to the brown book?" he asked instead, looking at Alice like she had suddenly grown a second head. Alice knew she hadn't because she could still see everything fine and she hadn't eaten anything since she got in here.

"I got rid of it," Alice said. "No one can read it anymore."

"Can you do it again?"

Alice stared at him for a long moment, trying to figure out if he was serious. He looked genuine, but she remembered everything that book had cost her. Even as her only hope, she had to get rid of it so that she could have time to continue looking for people lost, in a way, because of it. She had never been afraid of hearts before this, but now when she got too nervous, the beating hearts came back to her mind and she could feel them closing in around her. There was nothing about the experience that she wanted to repeat, but Peter kept looking at her like she was his only hope.

"No," Alice said after a long moment. "I'm busy right now. I'm looking for a couple lost boys."

"Oh, most of them are in Neverland. They didn't follow me through to… Wonderland, you said it was called? That's a really weird name."

"What?" Alice asked. "No, there's a couple boys from my school that ended up in Wonderland thanks to that damn Cat and I've been trying to find them. They're a bit taller than you, dark hair, brown eyes, probably making money off of people who don't know what they're in for or pulling pranks because they're bored. Can you tell me if you see them?"

"School?" he asked, thinking on the word hard. "I think I've heard about that. They have those in Wonderland?"

"I'm not from Wonderland," Alice told him, hopping off the bridge. "I live at Lucena Academy right now. And I need to get back there before anyone misses me."

"But aren't you here to save Wonderland?" he asked, that hope in his voice starting to wane. "And if you're going to save Wonderland, can't you save Neverland too? You already figured out how to save Wonderland, right? So now you can save Neverland for me."

"I'm just here to find Adam and Matt," she said. "Or Mark and Matt. I'm just here to find those two, and then I'm getting out of here forever. Wonderland has already caused me more than enough trouble as it is and I'll be glad when I never have to come back again. No one telling me how rude I am, no one inviting me to parties and not letting me drink the terrible tea. I'll be done and I can go back to normal again."

"If you don't want to save Wonderland anymore, then, we can switch!" he suggested, perching himself up on the edge of the bridge. "If I'm saving them, no one's going to try to tell me I'm rude. They're just going to know I'm a hero that saved them. And I can take down a wicked queen easy! I've gone up against Captain Hook so many times and won and he's a *pirate!* Some queen isn't going to be any match for me!"

"Is Captain Hook the guy who ruined Neverland?" Alice asked. "Did he get a book and start taking doing bad things there too?"

Peter sank at the mention of the book, the fear clouding over his face once more. "No," he said. "No, it wasn't him. But it's okay! You can do it and save Neverland! I've saved it so many times that it will be easy. So easy even a girl can do it." He laughed, though he didn't sound confident. "Besides, you were almost done here, right? So you're going to get bored if you don't do something else."

Alice frowned at him. She was not going to save Neverland for him. She didn't even want to save Wonderland. She was just here to get Adam and Matt out. She wasn't here to save anyone from the queen or put hearts back or close doors to keep mice out of the kitchen, or whatever else everyone thought she was doing here.

"I'm leaving," Alice said. "Don't go see the Queen. She's dangerous."

With that, she fell backwards off of the bridge. Peter watched her and didn't stop her as she fell through the surface of the water and out of Wonderland.

ALICE TUMBLED OUT of the mirror and landed on the floor with a heavy thud. The room was light as the day started to pour in and she could hear Adrianna in the washroom already. With a look at her wrist, the watch confirmed that it was already morning. She kicked off her shoes and crawled under the covers, ready for this day to be over.

She ignored the knock on the door, keeping her eyes firmly shut. Sleep was already coming for her as Adrianna padded across the room and opened it, letting Heather in.

"Oh, is Alice still sleeping? Sorry."

"I'll just be a minute," Adrianna told her quietly.

Heather let out a soft laugh. "Must have been a good night. Alice didn't even change."

Sleep was a mercy.

CHAPTER 9

Alice's Dating Troubles

THE PLAY LOOKED like it was going to be really good this year. The only plays she had been to were ones that Ms. Miller had taken her to relating to her course work. She had seen things like *Hamlet* and *Romeo and Juliet*, but that was nothing like their school's production of *Sweeney Todd*. There were songs and dancing, and so many things that the performers had to remember to do that Alice couldn't help but be impressed by it all. Even if she'd now seen them rehearsing so many times that she thought she might be able to recite the play from memory. Not that she minded. It was better than being out there.

"Hello again," Heather said, dropping into a seat next to Alice. "How's it going today? Has Kevin screwed up at all yet?"

Alice shook her head and put her homework down.

"Everyone's been doing really good. I thought they weren't doing your scene today."

"They aren't," she said with a wide smile. "I came looking for you."

Dread welled up in her at those words. "Me?" Alice asked. "Did Robert need a hand with something?"

"No." The smile widened. "Nike was asking if I knew where you were. He's been looking for you since classes got out."

"Oh." Alice kept her eyes on the stage, though it looked like they were wrapping up for the day.

"I don't think I've ever seen you this nervous around someone before, Alice," Heather told her. "He already likes you, though. You don't have to be so shy. You've already gone out with him."

"Yeah..." Alice risked a glance over at Heather, who was smiling and looking at her like she was able to read Alice like a book. As far as Heather was concerned, Nike liking Alice was the best thing that could have happened. She looked so happy about it that Alice couldn't bring herself to correct her yet.

"He can be a bit intimidating," Heather offered. "I mean, he knows all those people. His dad works in Hollywood, so he's actually been to parties with celebrities. But you're awesome too, and he knows that. That's why he likes you." She offered Alice a playful nudge. "No reason to avoid him like this. If you keep doing it, he might think you don't like him."

Good. Alice couldn't bring herself to say it. Heather was so happy about it that she didn't want to ruin it. She took a quiet breath and smiled, hoping that was all. She looked to the stage, seeing Kevin was already grabbing his things and heading up the aisle, so she did the same, hoping that Heather would let her go.

Heather laughed and leaned in next to her. "Kevin thinks you don't like him," she told Alice. "But that's stupid. Who wouldn't like him, right?"

"Right," Alice said. There was something to that. He wasn't *bad* and other people seemed to like him just fine. Maybe she just wasn't giving him a fair chance. Her being with him, even this little, had made Adrianna and Heather so happy that it might be worth spending a little more time with him. Maybe he wasn't actually as annoying as she kept remembering.

"Hey," Kevin said, checking his watch. "Sorry we ran a bit long. We gotta go."

"Go?" Heather asked.

"Go," Alice said. "We've got club. Sorry." She got up and Heather let her out, Alice falling in step next to Kevin as he set a brisk pace for the two of them to get out of there.

They said nothing as they walked across campus, Kevin

slowing their pace as soon as they were out of the theatre. Alice knew that they were in no hurry, neither of them having to report for library duty for another half hour. The rehearsals had even ended right on time.

"He won't come," Kevin said as they got to the building. "Nike? He's not coming to a library, even to visit you."

Alice nodded. "He's not that bad," she said. "He's just... I don't know."

"Well, he's probably going to be there tonight for the study session. It might be easier with everyone else there. And you better be there."

Alice nodded. Adrianna had been asking why she wasn't around for them, Robert messaged her late the previous night asking for help with homework. People were starting to notice she wasn't around as much anymore and they were starting to worry.

"Do you even like him?" Kevin asked as they got their first stack of books to put away. "I know the girls all seem to think he's great—"

"He's nice," Alice said. It was more for her own benefit than his. "I just need to give him a chance. He likes me, right? So I should at least try to like him too." Kevin looked like he wanted to say something, but he couldn't find the words. Alice kept her eyes on the shelves and the books. "Everyone says he's great and I'm lucky. And sometimes it just takes time before you realize you like someone."

She was annoyed and irritated at him, but it was probably because they were out on a Saturday when she wanted to be in Wonderland. She was upset about not being able to look for Adam and Matt and that had put her in a bad mood for the whole evening. Avoiding him was silly and she needed to stop that. It wasn't fair to him and she wasn't really trying to get to know him.

Kevin tugged her back as she wandered, stopping her from running into someone. She looked up, finding Travis looking down at her just as surprised to see her. "Oh, Alice. Hey."

"Hi," she said. "Sorry. I wasn't paying attention."

He smiled at her. "I hear Lance's been meddling," he said. "I hope you aren't letting him get away with too much."

"I don't think he's been getting in any trouble."

"You mean setting her up?" Kevin asked at the same time.

"I mean setting you up," Travis said, glancing back at Kevin. "Addie tells me you guys had fun."

"Yeah," Alice said. He kept looking over her to Kevin, and Alice put another book away. "Were you looking for something?"

"It's fine, Joe knows where the books are. So tell me about this guy."

"Nike?" Alice asked. She really wanted to not say anything about him just yet, not trusting her opinion. "He's nice."

"Nice?"

Alice nodded, but didn't meet his eyes.

Travis' eyes flickered back over to Kevin before he offered her a grin. "So long as he's nice," he said. "But look, there's something your sister used to tell me when she was around. You don't have to stick around just because he's nice. If you don't like him, you can say no."

Alice studied him carefully as he spoke, her mind catching on one thing. "You knew my sister?"

"Uh… yeah," he said, looking embarrassed. "We were in the same year. I thought I mentioned that before. Didn't I say that?"

She watched him stumble through his words, not sure why he was so embarrassed about it. With everything going on, she must have just forgotten he said anything. She did know that they were in the same year, after all, but with Wonderland and everything else, she'd been so distracted.

"Trav!" Joe called through the library, passing them in the shelves before turning back and catching his brother by the shoulder. Joe had gone back to looking like a student again, and it was a little weird to see him without the spikes after the holidays. "Hey Alice. Sorry, we have a paper to finish, so I'm going to need him back."

"Apparently the guy Lance found for her is *nice*," Travis told him.

"And that means you aren't interfering in your little sister's best friend's love life, right?" Joe said, dragging him off. "Come on, you are not leaving me with all the work on this again."

Alice watched the two of them leave until Kevin nudged her back toward the stacks. "Did I tell you about my break?" he asked, smiling as he started to tell her about his trip to Thailand with his mother and older sister. Alice listened as they went through the rest of the books, happy for the break. She forgot that he had a sister, though from the sound of it, they didn't get along very well at the moment.

The rest of the time passed quickly and they grabbed something from the cafeteria to eat on the way over to the dorms where everyone else was already in the midst of their study session. Kevin took the spot next to Nike and Alice settled down between Adrianna and Heather, getting her books out and trying to remember what she hadn't done already while she was watching the rehearsals.

With Wyatt helping Adrianna and Heather working her way easily through her assignments, Alice kept her head down at first and skimmed through her papers for anything she hadn't done. From the look of everything, she'd completed what she needed for the week already. She wanted to head back upstairs to her room, but she said she was going to be here.

"That doesn't look right." Alice looked up as Nike took a page of math homework and looked it over. "I think you forgot to carry something."

Alice looked over at the sheet. "No," she said, her eyes crawling over the equation and checking her math. "Seven and two only make nine. And then you divide by seven."

"There should be a remainder."

"Not on that one."

"That doesn't look right," he muttered, looking the problem over again with a pen in hand. She took her homework back from him and offered him a scrap of paper to work on instead. He looked at her, but accepted it and started working through the problem. Across the table, Heather gave her an encouraging smile.

Try to give him a chance, Alice told herself. He was only trying to help. And it wasn't like he said she was wrong, just that he thought it looked off.

She let him work through the problem and got up. Robert looked like he was having trouble with something and, as soon as she got over there, she saw that he was. He welcomed her help and she worked with him through the chapter first on Ancient Greece, going over what was important and making sense of the scramble of notes he'd taken in class. Alice relaxed into the old pattern; Kevin joining her on his other side to offer a note here or there, and Robert was starting to understand the material.

When it seemed that he was all right, Alice headed back to her seat, but Adrianna caught her before she got there and pulled her aside. She was blushing and wouldn't meet Alice's eyes, though kept a firm grip on her elbow. "Hey, do you want to go for a walk?" she asked.

"Sure," Alice said. "Is there something wrong?"

Adrianna shook her head. "I just… Wyatt and Nike thought that since everyone seems to be about done anyway, we could get some air together."

Alice looked over to the two of them taking, Nike looking back and giving her a smile. She returned it, feeling her back straighten a little and nodding to Adrianna. "Yeah," she said. She'd avoided him again and hadn't given him a chance. She needed to give him a chance. "Let's do that."

Alice and Adrianna went to grab their bags and their respective boys before leaving the table. Heather gave Alice another encouraging smile as they headed out the doors. She would give him a try. Maybe his stories were actually interesting if she really listened to them. She knew he was nice. Other people said nice things about him. She just had to give him a chance.

Alice wondered why Adrianna was still so nervous about

hanging out with Wyatt. She seemed to comfortable with him when they were actually out. When Wyatt was around, she barely paid attention to anyone else. Maybe she was just nervous about that first part where they were just starting to be alone, since they were quick to make their way ahead once they were out the doors.

"It's nice to see you again," Nike said, smiling at Alice. "Outside of class, I mean. I was getting worried you were avoiding me."

Alice laughed, remembering that she was supposed to do that. "No," she said. "I was just…"

"It's okay," he said. "Adrianna and Heather said you like to disappear sometimes and I shouldn't take it personally. Though maybe if you're heading off on your own a lot, maybe you'd like a little company."

Alice forced a smile. "Maybe," she said. Her mind was already wandering away from this conversation. She wondered if she could get a table and chair onto that rooftop garden. There was no door and no way anyone would be able to find her there. Maybe she could get a tent and hide there forever.

But she was going to try to get to know him better. This time he was actually interested in her. He was making an effort to get to know her, which was a good change. It would be nice if he asked her about something she wanted to talk about, but it was a start. He was trying and she would do the same.

"Where do you go, anyway?" he asked.

"You know," she said, gesturing with her hands to nowhere in particular. "Places. I get lost a lot."

"Then it's a good thing I have an excellent sense of direction. There's this trick I learned from one of the trainers out in Hollywood. He works on all the films where you get lost in the forest as a consultant and there's a few really easy ways you can use to find your way again."

Alice tried to listen, but nothing he said about moss growing on trees or the sun made any difference in Wonderland. Continuing to smile and taking care to nod when he paused, Alice tuned him out and she let her mind wander to her plans once she got back to the dorms. She typically spent her Sunday evenings on trying to decode the brown book. She was making slow progress so far, but there was still progress.

"We should go for dinner again, off campus," Nike suggested as they looped back around to the dorms again. Wyatt and Adrianna were back in step next to them, though Alice wasn't sure when that happened. "It was fun last time. There's another place in that strip mall that we should try too. Apparently it's Japanese. What about next Friday? I can make the reservations."

"We have exams next week, Nike," Wyatt said. "And the week after. Maybe when we're all done, though? To celebrate?"

"It sounds great," Adrianna said, looking hopefully to Alice.

"Yeah," Alice agreed, her ability to pretend that she was interested perfected over years of lying. "Sounds like fun. I don't think I've ever had Japanese before."

"You should try some of the sushi in the cafeteria to prepare," Nike suggested. "It's not as good as you get at a restaurant, of course, but you'll have a better idea of it when we get there."

"Do they do all you can eat?" Wyatt asked.

"You don't do all you can eat if you want the good stuff," Nike chided him. "If you want it to actually be good, you have to order it separately. They just use the garbage stuff for all you can eat. They can't make that much off of it, so why bother using the high quality stuff, right?"

Alice was sure she was in for another adventure in dining. Sushi, as she learned before she decided never to try it in the cafeteria, was uncooked fish. She was pretty sure you cooked fish to get rid of salmonella. Maybe she was missing something, and she would be sure to look it up tonight rather than ask why anyone would want to eat it raw. Apparently it was a Japanese thing.

"Oh, and before I forget," Nike said, reaching into his pocket. "I saw this and I thought of you. I hope you like it."

He handed Alice a small box and she put a smile on her face. She didn't want a gift from him. When someone gave you a gift, it was polite to do what they asked as a thanks. But it was a nice gesture, and he was a nice person. Maybe he wouldn't expect anything from it.

"You didn't have to," she said, trying to sound grateful.

"Of course I did," he said. "Open it."

Alice opened the box and part of her was upset about the beauty of it. It was a small heart with a couple diamonds set in it on a light silver chain. Something delicate, but not so fancy that she couldn't wear it with her uniform. She should be pleased, and she tried to make sure she looked like she was.

"It's so pretty," she said, and it was the truth.

"Here," he said, picking it up out of the box for her and in both hands. "Let me." Alice let him put it on her, moving her hair out of the way as he fumbled with the clasp. She put her hair down and he smiled expectantly at her. "Do you like it?"

"It's pretty. Thank you."

He smiled and leaned forward too quickly for her to react. He planted a kiss on her cheek and Alice flushed, though she wasn't sure why. She knew that she was supposed to blush when a boy kissed her. She'd seen that on television. But, between this and the gift, it also felt like she was being claimed.

They shared an awkward laugh as he backed away. Alice didn't know what she was supposed to say and he looked down

at his feet. "Sorry," he said before taking her hand. "We should catch up with Wyatt," he said and he pulled her along with him into the dorms.

Alice was glad when they said goodbye for the night, heading back into their room without Nike trying to kiss her again and Adrianna looking like her heart was melting from happiness. She had clearly had a much better night than Alice had.

"How's Wyatt?" Alice asked, the smile she'd kept plastered on her face softening into a real one.

"He's perfect," she said, her voice wistful and looking out into the depths of their room as she sank on her bed. "He asked me if he could kiss me and I said yes! It was so wonderful. It was perfect!"

At least her kissing experience went better. Adrianna was so busy feeling happy about everything that had happened that she didn't ask Alice about how her alone time with Nike went. That was fine by Alice, heading to her dresser and making sure she changed into something more comfortable for the rest of the evening. Adrianna barely noticed until Alice took off the necklace.

"What's that?" she asked darting over to look at it.

"Nike gave it to me."

"It's so pretty!" Adrianna said. "You're so lucky."

"Yep," Alice said, tying her hair back with an elastic and perching up on her chair. She wanted to work through the brown book. There weren't too many images left to go through at this point for this chapter. It was still on mythical beasts, but she needed to at least make sure all these pages belonged to this section before she did any real deciphering. There was so much left to do on this thing that she wasn't sure that she would have time to get it all done before school was out.

"Wyatt asked if we could go for sushi on Friday anyway," Adrianna said. "I said I'd check with you first."

"Sure," Alice said, too distracted by the book to think about how much she dreaded a meal of raw fish and unfortunate company.

CHAPTER 10

Castle in the Sky

JAPANESE FOOD WAS good, but the company left Alice wanting to leave. Nike gave her another gift, this time a pair of earrings that he didn't insist Alice try on immediately. Again, they were pretty and Alice was starting to get used to receiving things from him. It was like a reward for spending time with him, but they weren't making her like him. She just couldn't make herself like him.

Still, it was Friday night, so she went into the mirror once they got back. Alice didn't know how much longer she was going to be able to handle pretending she liked Nike as much as she was supposed to. The gifts made it uncomfortable and she knew that they meant that she was supposed to like him more, but it wasn't working.

"*Ábedecian gamenian snytrian eormencynn hércyme!*" she called out in the grass of Wonderland before falling back and staring up in the sky, looking at the one cloud as it floated overhead. She wondered idly how it moved when there wasn't a breeze, but it drifted through the sky without much difficulty. It was a little odd, but no odder than anything else. And it was generous enough to not drift over her, so she was grateful for that.

She let the memories of the date fall away. Nike wouldn't be able to find her in Wonderland. She considered just staying here for a while and taking the whole weekend off of seeing anyone. She could, and sleep through Sunday. There was only Library, but she doubted anyone would notice if she missed a week.

Her trips to Wonderland were getting stranger and stranger of late. Eyes found her wherever she turned up and people stopped her. They all brought friends or family who just sat there, staring at their heart and wouldn't do anything else. Though Alice did her best to return them, finding she was less scared the more she worked with the hearts, she realized she had gained a reputation as someone who could fix their problems.

Well, so long as they had their own heart. There was nothing she could do if they held the wrong one.

She enjoyed her momentary solitude, but she knew it was only a matter of time before they came to her again. It didn't matter where she was, they would always find her. Sometimes one or two, sometimes a crowd. They paid her in momentary compliments and little else. After all, she was the only person in Wonderland who knew how to put hearts back. Clearly it was her job to be doing this, and one should not be thanked for a job they are required to do.

It was strange that none of them could tell her how they got their hearts back. They only seemed to remember losing them, then regaining them. That would be enough, except Alice wanted to know where they were all coming from.

And then there were those rounding them back up to bring back to the Queen. She saw the force expand beyond cards, which were now being kept closer to the castle. Other creatures, bears and larger beasts, were coming out to reclaim the hearts with the same dead eyes that their victims had. They carried the hearts on their backs, all of them beating as one and making the bag pulse as they carried them away, a whole fleet of heartless victims in tow.

Sometimes Alice thought about stealing the bag and seeing how many hearts she could send in one go, if she even could. However, she had no desire to fight a bear in order to get them, so the idea was very quickly dropped in exchange for something more practical: Asking if any of them had seen a lost boy.

None of them had seen a boy, but a few of those who had not had hearts stolen spoke of a crazy flying child that liked to play tricks and laugh at them. They were having quite the time keeping him away from their things, which he liked to look at and sometimes steal if they looked particularly interesting. She was fairly certain she had met this laughing boy that reminded everyone of a very obnoxious chickadee.

"Fancy meeting you here!"

Speaking of, Peter Pan appeared above her, looking down with his long dark hair hanging over his eyes as he smiled. He was horizontal in the air, and flipped upside down to float next to her, just above the grass with his hands behind his head.

"Hello Peter," Alice said, not in an unfriendly way, and she sat up. "I hear you've been annoying the people of Wonderland. Could you please try to not steal anything more from them? They say that you've got a particular fondness for thimbles and their sewing is starting to fall behind. Though I'm not sure what they're sewing right now."

"I've only been stealing kisses!" Peter said in his own defence, though Alice didn't see how that was any better. "And Wonderland is boring. Tiger Lily won't talk to me. None of the Lost Boys have found me yet. And you don't come by often enough to do anything!"

"Were you really looking for me?" Alice asked.

"I'm so bored, I'm willing to play with a girl!" Peter said. He was positively exasperated and Alice smiled a little as she shook her head. Peter was more like a little kid in the way he was irritating compared to Nike, so it was not as annoying to her anymore. Plus, she'd learned how to make him shut up now.

"If you're so bored, you could always go rescue your Lost Boys from Neverland," she suggested. "Didn't you say you were the hero of Neverland and would save everyone? You should really probably get started on that."

Peter looked defiantly back at her. He didn't seem to be so bothered by the mention of Neverland anymore. "Shouldn't you be saving Wonderland instead of just lying on the grass?" he asked. "Or finding those boys you lost? What kind of girl can't even keep track of the boys who are supposed to be protecting you? You left yourself wide open for an attack!"

He lunged forward at her with his sword and she disappeared. She appeared behind him, tapping him on the shoulder. When he swung around, she was gone, appearing behind him again with a smile. She waited quietly as he kept whipping his head back and forth to find her.

"I seem to be able to avoid an attack fine on my own," she said, Peter swinging around to her again. She reached behind her as she spoke and plucked the sword out of his hand, holding it before him now. She grinned as he looked down at his hand to find nothing there. She offered back his sword and he snatched it away from her, pouting as he put it back in his belt. "Tiger Lily is just really good at surprising me."

"No fair," he said. "You're cheating by disappearing like that."

"Then stop flying," Alice said, knowing he wouldn't. He crossed his arms and turned away from her in the air. It was nice actually being able to talk back. No consequences like making a boy break up with you, or getting threatened with doctors. There was only maybe the threat of a lecture, and Peter was not capable of delivering one of those.

"And I think I've already done a decent job of helping Wonderland," Alice continued. "No more book, returning hearts here and there. Everyone's already getting their hearts back on their own even. And what have you done for Neverland so far? I mean, besides running away?"

She saw him grab his arms more tightly at that and she knew she'd struck a chord. Tiger Lily's tribe had run from whatever Neverland had become. They said they escaped, though Alice didn't know where Neverland was, or if it bordered Wonderland at all. It had to be close, but Alice wondered if perhaps they had to take a boat. She had no idea where they came from or how they fit in Wonderland, or if they could even exist in the same space as Wonderland since they didn't make sense in the nonsense.

"Yeah, well at least *I can fly*," he said finally, trying to look defiant. "Flying is way better than disappearing. I can go wherever I want, even up into the castle up there!"

He pointed up to the single cloud in the sky that was now slowly floating away. Alice looked at it, her mind starting to work already and she wondered.

"Castle?" she asked. Was there something up there that she didn't know about? She certainly hadn't looked in the sky for anyone. It could have been a place where one of the boys had landed. If it was in the sky, they wouldn't be able to get down. And she had seen someone float down from somewhere. She knew it was Adam or Matt, so what if they had come from up there? What if one of them was still up there?

"You didn't know about the castle?" he asked, laughing again. "I thought you were supposed to be the hero here, but I should have known better. Girls are too busy being pretty and girly to do hero stuff."

"Just tell me about the castle," she snapped at him.

"It's a great big castle in the sky!" he said. "There's only birds inside and all of them yell really loudly. I don't know what they're talking about, but their king doesn't like me that much. I told them that birds were the ones who taught me to fly, but I don't know what he said after that. They yell so loud that you can't even hear anything afterwards. And there's a bird that carries the whole thing on its back. It's not a cloud up there, just a storm crow. It's made of clouds and when it's upset, it makes storms rain down. Apparently it only happens when they get visitors."

It figured that there would be a castle of birds up there. The castle was probably made entirely of clouds, too, and still the Mad Hatter would probably find a way to have tea there. She would need to check to see if he had seen any sign of the boys soon, but she needed to check this out first.

As if he could read her intentions, Peter picked her up and lifted her with him into the sky. "Come on!" he said. "How are you going to save Wonderland if you haven't even seen all of it?"

"You can't just pick people up and fly them places," Alice told him, though she didn't mind the lift. If there was a chance that Adam or Matt was up there, she was willing to be dragged around by the armpits to strange places in the sky. "At the very least, ask! It's really rude!"

Peter laughed at that. "Rude! Now you sound like you're from Wonderland! Where's your sense of adventure, Alice? Why do girls never have that? Tiger Lily never wanted to come exploring with me either."

"Tiger Lily has people to watch," Alice said. "And people to hold hostage in a tent."

Peter laughed at that too. "She told me about that one. It sounds like she's really good at keeping you from disappearing. Her father wanted to keep you as a witch and use you to make a fortune for himself. You can't trust the Indians, Alice. They're loyal, but only after they like you. Like they like me."

"I just want them to leave me alone," Alice told him. "So far, Tiger Lily has been trying to catch me and she's a little too good at it. I need to figure out how to escape her. And the Red Knight. And the Queen of Hearts. And Nike."

"Maybe if you challenge them to combat," Peter suggested. "Well, if you win against Tiger Lily, then you'll become the new princess of the Indians."

"I really don't want to be a princess," Alice said. Peter laughed and looked questioningly down at her, but she rolled her eyes. "Long story. The Queen of Hearts really wants a pretty little daughter."

"And that's you?" he asked. He didn't sound like he believed it, but he didn't linger on it. "Tiger Lily is kinda sorry about what she did, though. To you. She said she wanted to apologize and ask for your help again, but you never stick around long enough to talk."

"Well, maybe if she didn't kidnap me in the first place, I'd be a little more open to talking to her." They were getting closer to the cloud, but Alice was mulling over Peter's words. She didn't trust Tiger Lily to just talk. She had escaped from her for a reason. That reason was forced imprisonment and drugging that had taken her over a week to heal from and her life had fallen apart.

"You can't still be mad about that," he said as they got closer to the cloud. "It happened ages ago!"

The cloud palace was just as she imagined. The storm crow that held the cloud looked more and more like a normal white bird the closer they got. Riding on its back was a castle that looked like it was made of columns of clouds. There was no one outside, but Alice could already hear them from up here. They sounded like very loud winds and she couldn't make out what was going on.

"Maybe you should ask them to teach you to fly," Peter suggested, raising his voice to be heard over the loud wind now whipping past their ears. "I can't keep carrying you everywhere forever."

Alice didn't know what to say to that as he dropped her down on the cloud ground. Her feet did not fall through, though they made an unpleasant sound as they landed. She let out an apology out of habit, which seemed to placate what-ever made the sound, though Peter looked at her funny. "It's polite," she told him.

She led the way, Peter trailing behind and poking at the ground as he actually walked on it. He rushed ahead of her after a moment, and almost let himself into the front doors of the palace. Alice reached out and stopped him, not wanting him to be rude to whoever the rulers of this place were.

"You can't just walk in," she told him. "This isn't like Neverland. There's rules here."

"Why?" he asked, moving to open the doors again. She

grabbed his hands again and pushed them away, knocking on the door instead.

A small panel on the door opened and there was a small bald bird staring out at them. There was less wind here and they didn't need to talk so loudly, though the bird put his beak right up into the window to speak to them. "Who goes there and what business have you with the palace?"

Alice had no idea why he needed to be so loud. She winced at the volume, but managed to keep her composure. Peter stuck his finger in his ear as if it were going to dig out the faint ringing that the bird's voice left behind.

"Hello," Alice said, clearly though she was careful not to yell. Her voice sounded quiet in her own ears and she wondered if anyone could even hear her. She dipped into a curtsy despite Peter rolling his eyes next to her. "My name is Alice. I am here looking for a couple of my friends. They have gotten lost and I wanted to ask if you or anyone else present in the palace had seen them."

The bird's eyes moved over her and he was patient in looking her over this time. He seemed satisfied with Alice, though his eye went much longer over Peter and he looked far less satisfied with what he saw there. Where Alice was dressed still in several pieces from her date, replacing the shoes and removing the jewelry, she was still nicely put together. Peter, on the other hand, with his patchwork of clothing, looked out of place.

The bird moved his eyes out of the window and brought his mouth back up to it. "What is that with you?"

Peter looked like he was going to say something and Alice put a hand over his mouth before he could utter a word. He tried to pry it off his face, but Alice kept it there as she talked. "His name is Peter. He is my helper in trying to find them. There are two of them you see, and it takes two people to find two people. Otherwise, I might find one and miss the other."

The bird took a moment to consider this, staring at her through the window again. Alice did not remove her hand from Peter's mouth and, in a way that was the exact opposite of grabbing a cupcake from across the cafeteria, dropped her arm down to her side. Peter struggled against her disembodied hand, but Alice kept her grip tight.

The bird saw nothing bizarre about this and nodded. "You may enter," he said, letting the doors open to reveal the small bird with the large voice and big beak standing just on the other side, much too short to actually be up to the level of the hole in the door. Alice curtsied to it and yanked Peter down with her hand to bow before she let go. She shot him a warning look to stay quiet and smiled at the bird.

"Thank you so very much for admittance," she said.

"You should see the court face maker," he said, his voice

even louder now that she was next to him. "He will make the face of the one you are looking for and you can show that instead of telling them what these boys you have lost look like. It will be much easier for them to figure out if they have seen them that way."

"Thank you," Alice said. "Have you seen them? There's two boys, a little older than I am. They are about this tall with dark hair. They like to play jokes on people or trick them into doing things for them."

The bird at the gate thought for a moment about it. "I have not seen two boys fitting this description," he said in such a way that Alice had to wonder about it. Peter kept looking around like he was about to fly off, but she shot him a warning look to behave, which he was obeying for the moment. She had to thank him for at least managing to behave himself this much. She had the feeling it was difficult for him.

"Have you seen *one* boy fitting that description?" she asked.

"Oh yes," the bird said. Alice was finding herself grateful that he was so loud because she couldn't even hear her own voice anymore. For all she knew, Peter was busy saying many rude things behind her and she had gone deaf to him. "I saw the one, though quite a while ago."

"You did?" Alice said, quite hopeful.

"Oh yes," the bird said. "I don't know what happened to him. He was taken to see the king. Very rude, that one. Kept shouting and yelling. No manners at all. Said that we didn't know our manners. I don't imagine the king liked him much. Would you believe he pushed the doors open without knocking first?"

Alice did her best to look shocked, though said nothing. She shot a look at Peter, who rolled his eyes and stayed in step beside her. He didn't look like he was saying anything yet, though she was sure that this bird would tell her as soon as he let anything slip out, whether she could hear Peter or not.

"Do you know of anyone who might know what happened to him?" she asked.

"Well, I suppose he would be the best person to tell you what happened to him," the bird said, contemplating. "I don't believe he left a name."

"I am having a bit of trouble finding him at the moment," Alice said. "Is there perhaps another person who would know where he'd gone?"

"Oh, the King of the Skies would know," he said. "He knows everything about the people who come and go through here. A bit loud, though, if you ask me. Come along, this way."

Alice followed the small bird and Peter followed after her, continuing to pick at his ear to get the ringing out. He was ready to cover them again the next time anyone tried to talk and Alice couldn't blame him for it. She just hoped their attention stayed on her and not on Peter for now, which seemed to be working so far as they entered the cloud throne room.

There was a very regal looking bird dressed in colourful feathers perched atop a very intricate, gilded perch next to a much plainer bird on a less regal perch. Both were preening themselves right up until Alice and Peter entered, to which they ruffled their feathers and turned sharply to the entrants.

"Who goes there?" the bird Alice assumed was the King asked, his voice loud and booming, even more so than the one that had let them in.

"Presenting Alice and Peter," the bird said, Peter wincing next to her. Alice kept her hands down and folded in front of her. Well, one hand. She could see Peter's mouth opening beside her and slipped her other hand over his mouth to keep him quiet. He looked more angry with her than anything else, but he followed her curtsy with a bow. The king beckoned them silently forward. She removed her hand.

"My king," Alice began getting up from her deep curtsy.

"What brings you before me?" he asked, looking her carefully over. His voice was loud and booming, and Alice was now completely unable to hear her own voice underneath his.

"I am looking for two boys," she said, very careful to make sure she wasn't shouting. She knew shouting would be rude, even if she couldn't hear what she was saying, and the sensation of it was completely wrong to her. "We have been told that one of them may have come through here. He is about this tall with dark hair. He may have been shouting a lot."

The king nodded knowingly. "I know the one you are looking for. He was rude and would not stop shouting, so we sent him to the dungeons to learn his lesson. He did not seem to like it much there, though."

"Please pardon my asking," Alice said, hoping that she wasn't interrupting a story and instead stopping one well before it happened. She had a lead at last and she didn't want to lose it. "Is he still there?"

The king shook his head. "He managed to escape. We aren't quite sure how. He never stopped shouting, but it was a pleasant change to not hear him any longer."

"Pardon me, but may I see where you kept him?" Alice asked. She was so close. He had been here. One of them had been here. She just needed to be sure, and maybe, just maybe, he might have left behind a sign so she could know which of the two of them it was.

"Take them," the King instructed a toucan lingering in the back of his court.

The toucan shuffled forward and led them away. He showed them down to the dungeons and Alice could see why anyone would want to escape. As loud as the people were, she could still hear the blinding winds that echoed in the dungeons. The rooms were large and warm with a view of Wonderland, but it was cacophonous and she couldn't keep herself from covering her ears.

Inside one room, she could see something scratched into the cloud that was still there for reasons that Alice couldn't make sense of, nor did she care to attempt to understand it. In the wall was *Adam Markus Case.* That was enough for Alice.

Peter tapped her on the shoulder and Alice smiled. She pointed at the cell and gave a thumbs up. Peter didn't seem to care about that at all and pointed down at the window. He then proceeded to fly off, back down into Wonderland.

Alice figured that this was longer than she could have hoped for him to stay with her already. She turned with a smile to the toucan and let herself down into a curtsy. "Thank you very much for your help," she said.

The toucan bowed back and said something, but Alice was gone when he rose again.

ALICE APPEARED IN the forest where she had seen Peter point to. She recognized it even from the sky. It was right at the small bridge where they had spoken before, and she beat him down. There wasn't much left to do today, but she found herself smiling that she had finally managed to make some progress. Even with her ears ringing, she had actually found a place where Adam had been once. It was more than she had gotten in a year of searching.

Peter joined her a moment later, smacking the side of his head and trying to get the sound of the ringing out. Alice knew it wasn't going to go away anytime soon, though it didn't stop her from laughing at how silly Peter looked. She smiled brightly and hugged him. Without him, she wouldn't have even thought to check the cloud.

He tried to say something and pushed her away, but Alice couldn't hear a word of it. He squirmed out of her grasp and flew away, though Alice wasn't bothered by it. She'd already been so lucky, even if it cost her hearing. Looking around, she dared to hope that the forest might give her something to make this trip even better. Maybe Adam would come out of the woods.

Instead, she only felt eyes on her. Eyes watching her. She was used to that now, but nothing came out of the woods for her. She looked back at them and took a step towards them, looking around for a moment before she went back to the bridge. It was strange. There would usually be people looking to her to return their hearts to them again, but they didn't come out this time.

There was nothing she could do about it today. She

couldn't have heard any requests made of her anyway. Before they changed their mind, she left Wonderland, hoping that her hearing would come back sooner than later.

CHAPTER 11

Jealousy Strikes

IT TOOK HER nearly a week to properly regain her hearing, which gave her a good reason to spend time alone instead of with anyone else, especially Nike. Now she wasn't off wandering, as far as he knew. She just didn't want to bore him with her inability to communicate after having Adrianna blow out her eardrums with too loud music blaring through her headphones.

With spring break coming up, Alice made very sure she was never alone with Nike. She was there at the study groups, but she took extra shifts at the library on the understanding that this meant she wouldn't have to come in while she was doing finals this year. It seemed she wasn't the only one, as there were a few people looking to fulfill their volunteer hours before their years got very busy.

Nike wanted to ask her something, but so far she was able

to avoid it. He'd been trying to find her when she disappeared. Heather told him about her spot in the theatre and, though it was dry enough now to sit out in the garden, she worried that he'd spot her out there. She moved herself into the dark back corner to watch the rehearsals of the play where no one else paid any attention to her.

Someone caught her back there once and asked her to leave. Alice remembered that particular cast member, the understudy for Mrs. Lovett, and was sure to avoid her. Alice was back in a few minutes later in a new spot she'd noticed on her way out. There was a catwalk that went over the audience that turned out to be comfortable enough. She sat up there during rehearsals so that the girl couldn't spot her again.

She did the same for when Heather was there. As part of the chorus with only one death scene, she was not there as often as Kevin was, and Kevin wasn't going to go telling Nike where she was hiding. As far as she knew, he hadn't even mentioned to Heather that Alice was still there. He'd also been the one to pipe up when she first started hiding in the back of the theatre saying that she was a friend of his.

It wasn't like the theatre was empty most of the time. The crew sat around between working on sets to watch the rehearsals as well. If asked, Alice would get up to help here and there, but for the most part she was a piece of the background.

She sat in the back of the theatre today with her laptop, trying to decipher the brown book and taking notes. She had the glow of the screen down as low as it would go, the rehearsal acting as background noise. She barely noticed if there was a sour note sung, a line flubbed, or if someone fell to the laughter of the rest of the cast. She was completely absorbed in her work. She only had a year left to either find the boys or to get rid of the Bandersnatch and, with the Bandersnatch's section so small and underdeveloped; she turned instead to the spells section.

She remembered parts of this section from her month in the tent much more clearly than the rest, even now. There were the names she could assign, and the true names. A true name was the one that would always work with them and the vocabulary she had been using for them so far were replacements. She could string as many words together as she wanted and try to make it as precise as possible, but she was never going to get it quite as accurate as if she used its actual name.

She'd figured out a few things already from working through these. If she used the genus and the scientific classifications of animals, the ones that heard her would come out to her. It was a bit better than the classifications in the book, though she started combining them a little so that it was the scientific names and a personality trait. Friendly birds were around the school and willing to come land on her head for a moment before flying off. It worked, as near as she could tell, though she kept from trying it on people so far.

It did rely on a certain understanding level, too. Simple creatures would be harder to call individually and more intelligent creatures would need to be called more specifically. The book was meant for those more intelligent creatures that they didn't have true names for. The vocabulary stretched on for pages, but she wasn't sure what other words she would put in with the Bandersnatch or with Adam and Matt. Still, she was picking the words out one by one and trying to put the pages back together just so she could look through her options.

She started to skip over the sections of vocabulary that she could use to try and describe the creatures should she encounter a new one and went back over the section on the Bandersnatch again. She knew there was nothing in there about his real name, but she always went back to it, hoping that there would be something in there that could help her figure out what it was. Carl or George or something simpler than what was written in this book, with all the strange accents and weird iterations of the characters that she hadn't seen before. Alice needed something in nice, simple English, but the creature was too old for that and she knew full well that she was going to be dealing with a name that was probably even older than the language in this book. The Bandersnatch had said that he was tricked before and was stronger now. She didn't doubt that he would have found another way to keep out of the book, maybe by even changing his name.

She went back to translating again, keeping the images in one window in their original form, and the editor in another trying to skew and change them around so she could read them. She wrote them out in the spare pages of a notebook that she long ago decided she didn't need to use for class. Math notes were unnecessary when everything was in the text book anyway, and their homework was all done on handouts and in booklets, not their own pages.

"So that's what you keep working on back here."

Alice slammed the laptop shut and spun around, finding Kevin on the chairs behind her and leaning over her shoulder to see what she was doing. He smiled at her, keeping his laughter in as she tried to keep her composure about her.

"I won't ask," he said, holding up his hands in defeat and smirking. "We're wrapping in about ten minutes. Figured you'd like to know."

"Thanks," she said.

"You *really* don't want to talk to Nike, do you?" he asked, looking around at the otherwise empty theatre. The crew had already gone home, calling it an early night for a job getting close to done. The sets were mostly built and the props taken care of. Now it was just a matter of maintenance and making sure the actors didn't break anything before the play. That, and making sure there were plenty of replacements for when they did inevitably break something or fall through it.

"It's not that," Alice said. She knew that she was supposed to be giving him a chance. He bought her nice things and he was funny and rich and well connected. She knew that she was supposed to like him. "I just…"

"Really don't want to talk to Nike," Kevin said. On stage, they were rehearsing a scene that did not involve him, so he did not need to be up there. He could have left already instead of visiting her back here. "It's okay. You don't like the guy. It kind of makes sense."

"What does?" she asked.

"Look," he said. "Heather thinks he's awesome because he knows famous people. *He* thinks he's awesome because he knows famous people. You didn't know *Back to the Future* last year."

Alice smiled half-heartedly. "He always talks about all these people like I'm supposed to know who they are," Alice said. "I just… I don't get it. Are they really that important? They act. I get that that's good. I just don't know why everyone else is so obsessed with them, though. It's just their job, right?"

He patted her on the head. "Oh Alice," he said. "So young. So naïve. You need Robert to teach you the ways of pop culture before you're ready to go out with a guy like Nike."

"Can't Heather just go out with him?" Alice asked. "She likes him. She likes gifts. She likes all this weird seafood he keeps wanting to go eat whenever we go out places."

"I think she's a little more interested in getting you to fall in love with him," he said. "She's got it in her head that you two are meant to be."

"What about Adrianna and Wyatt?"

"Not as interesting," Kevin said. "His family isn't as interesting or glamorous as Nike's is, so she isn't as interested. I'm not sure where she's gotten all this from. It's like she's turned into Sarah."

"What?" Alice asked, wide eyed and staring at Kevin.

"What?" he asked.

"Sarah," Alice said. "You said Sarah."

Kevin looked at her and blinked a few times. A wave of confusion passed over his face before it settled into a generally puzzled expression. "I did," he said. "Wasn't there a Sarah that used to go here? I can kind of remember someone named Sarah. From California or something?"

Alice stared at him as he tried to work it out. She could hardly believe that anyone remembered Sarah at all. She wanted — *needed* — to know if he remembered anything else. She put her laptop into her backpack and looked on stage to find that the rehearsals were done for the night. With everyone else heading home, Alice urged Kevin up to his feet.

"That's right," she said. "There was a girl named Sarah in our year back in first year. Blonde. She had a thing with makeup and matchmaking."

"That sounds right," he said. "Sarah. I don't know how I thought of her. I haven't seen her in a while. What happened to her? Transferred out? I just kind of don't remember her after a while, like she just left. Was she in our class or something?"

"Or something," Alice said. They went to the cafeteria, both of them needing to grab something to eat. Alice needed a snack at the very least, and she was glad to have the company. "No one else seems to remember Sarah."

"I didn't either," Kevin said. "It's weird. Don't tell anyone, but sometimes I can tell things that no one else really can. Like, remember things no one else seems to remember. There's a few people around campus. I know this is going to sound crazy, but I swear there have been a few people missing since that whole ghost thing last year."

"Really," Alice said, trying to keep calm on the outside. There was someone else who remembered.

They made it to the cafeteria and got burgers before grabbing a seat. Alice watched as his eyes searched around air and tried to find the memories he couldn't quite grasp. It was like when Ryan was trying to remember Adam and Matt before, like they were just escaping and he could almost feel them there. "Is there anything else strange?" she asked.

He looked at her suspiciously over his burger, eyes narrowed as he watched her. "You know something," he said. "You do, don't you? You remember Sarah."

"Well, yeah," she said. "We went to class with her all first year. Blonde girl, makeup obsessed. She danced with Robert."

"And now Heather's acting a bit like her," he said. "But I don't remember at all what she sounded like or looked like," he added. "She was blonde?"

Alice nodded. He kept looking at her and she stayed calm under his gaze. She knew he was trying to piece together his own memories more than focus on her.

"Why doesn't anyone else remember her?" he asked. "I don't think Robert's ever noticed her missing, but she sounds like the sort of girl he would have been drooling over. In fact, I'm sure he would have. But he doesn't seem to remember anyone like that."

"Maybe your memory is just better," Alice suggested.

"There's something else," he added, his mind switching and his eyes looking to one side before snapping back in to look at her again. "You. There was something that happened to you last semester, right? You were gone for a while and no one knew where you were."

"I'm always disappearing," Alice said, the lie coming easily though her mind was flying into a panic.

"There's nothing weird about me vanishing for a little while."

"It wasn't that," he said. "There were cops at school. I remember the cops. But no one else remembers the cops. Cops who kept asking about you."

"Do you really think I'd still be here if I had cops after me?" she asked. Her voice was light and joking, but she was worried that he might start remembering things she didn't want him to if she let him go for too long. She wished he would focus on things she could handle him remembering. "Come on, Kevin. This is a good school. If I were being hunted down by the cops and I'd disappeared, do you really think that my parents would ever let me come back here again?"

He pondered her words, but Alice didn't have time to get him back on track. There was another boy storming to their table, his footsteps heavy as they came closer. He stopped behind Kevin and towered over him, looking down at him furiously.

"Hello Nike," Alice said, a smile plastering itself to her face.

"What are you doing hanging out with him?" Nike demanded. The cafeteria was almost empty, but Alice felt like they were drawing eyes from every table. It was the tone her father would take with her when she had disappointed him. Like she had done something to personally wrong him.

"We were just getting dinner," Alice said. She knew that she had to be accommodating, but she wanted to keep talking to Kevin and see if there was anything else he could recall. Already, he knew more than Adrianna did. Unfortunately, Nike looked mad for some reason and she would have to placate him first.

"Why were you getting it with *him*?" Nike demanded, arms crossed. "You're *my* girlfriend."

"Because he's my friend," Alice told him. She was confused and she let that show on her face. She was careful not to raise her voice or get angry with him. He was angry, so she should be apologetic. She met his eyes and did her best to look sorry, her voice confused and remorseful. "I wasn't aware that I wasn't allowed to have dinner with friends."

"Yeah, back off," Kevin said, coming back to himself. "She can have dinner with whoever she wants."

"Are you trying to steal my girl?" he asked, looking narrow eyed down at Kevin.

Kevin turned around to look up at him, but kept his posture relaxed. He looked calm and cool and more confident than Alice knew he was feeling. Under the table, she could see he'd clenched his fist so tight that his nails dug into his hand.

"I'm just getting a meal with a friend," he said. "Is there something saying that I can't be her friend?"

"A guy and a girl are never just *friends*," Nike said. "It's not possible. You're trying to steal my girlfriend from me."

"Why would I try to steal your girlfriend?" he asked. "She likes you, doesn't she?"

Alice nearly choked on her fry, but managed to stay silent. She just watched, putting the food down. Part of her wanted to leave this situation, but that would only make it worse. She had to be kind and courteous so that Nike would not feel so angry, though she wasn't sure what he was talking about.

"Did you want to join us?" Alice asked. "There's room for one more."

"After you tried cheating on me?"

"What?"

"Did you think I wouldn't find out? I know you keep spending all that time sneaking off to watch the rehearsals. I bet you two have been going out behind my back this whole time!"

"No," Alice said, looking confused more than anything else. It was funny, but she knew that she shouldn't laugh at someone who was mad. That only made it worse. She just needed to be direct about it. "He's just a friend. I'm not dating Kevin. I go and watch them rehearse sometimes, but I don't want to go out with him."

"Just a friend," Kevin repeated. "Not a couple. She's not my type."

Nike glared between the two of them. "Fine," he said. "I still don't trust you." Kevin made a movement like he didn't care, but Nike turned to Alice. "I *was* going to invite you to come stay with my family over the break, but you keep disappearing on me. And now I catch you almost cheating on me, going off and having dinner with some guy without telling me first."

Alice knew that he wanted her to feel ashamed of her actions, so she tried to look as meek as possible. She didn't know why anything she had done was bad, but she knew that was the reaction he was looking for to avoid a scene. "Sorry," she said.

"You can't come anymore," he said. "I was going to introduce you to all sorts of people and you could have gone to all these parties with me, but now you're just going to have to think about what you did. Maybe when I get back, *maybe* I'll think about letting you come by in the summer. If you can prove yourself to me."

"Okay," Alice said, not quite meeting his eyes when she apologized. Her father didn't like it when she looked him in the eye and Nike was giving her the same feeling. She could see him nod and leave her there to feel bad for herself.

She kept her head down until he was gone. When she looked up, Kevin was staring at her. Alice no longer had that remorseful and sorry look on her face, instead letting her annoyance show through. Kevin laughed when he saw it, Alice staring at where Nike had disappeared off to instead of at Kevin.

"Prove myself to him to what?" she asked after a moment, annoyed and confused. "I don't even know what just happened. Why was he mad?"

"Because he thought I was stealing his woman," Kevin said, laughing.

"But I don't even *want* to be his woman!" she said. "I don't get this dating stuff. Heather can have him."

Kevin laughed and let her rant as they finished up before heading back to the dorms. Alice, if nothing else, felt better by the end, but Kevin was still laughing about it. He tried to explain her that Nike was just a possessive jerk, but Alice couldn't understand what was so bad about just having dinner with friends.

Dating, Alice decided, was too much trouble. She was only going out with him so that Adrianna didn't have to go out on dates with Wyatt alone, but if this was what she needed to deal with, she was going to make Adrianna go on her own. She already liked Wyatt and they ended up going off on their own anyway once they were out. She didn't need Alice there.

And then Alice could go back to focusing on finding her brothers. She didn't have much time and she was wasting too much of it dealing with Nike.

"He didn't ask if you had plans for the break," Kevin noted. "And it's in, like, two days. How were you going to get out of what you were doing to go with him?"

Alice shook her head and shrugged as they headed back to the dorms. "I don't know. I guess going to Hollywood was supposed to be so awesome that I was willing to drop everything to go with him to meet a bunch of famous people I don't know."

"That could be a great book. *Famous People I've Never Heard Of*, a story by Alice Liddell."

Alice gave him a sour look and he laughed, backing off like he thought she might hit him. "So what were you doing for the break anyway?" he asked. "Are you going anywhere?"

"You could say that," Alice said.

CHAPTER 12

The Edge of Wonderland

ORIGINALLY, ALICE WAS supposed to go home for the break, but her father had contacted her to tell her she would be staying at school. He had a trip and said he had informed the school already, though she remained on the list of students returning home.

She told Adrianna the evening before the break where she would actually be. It wasn't a surprise to know Alice was going into Wonderland to look for her brothers, but it was news that Alice had a lead. Adrianna wished her luck as she passed through the mirror, though she still insisted that she didn't need to work so hard to bring them back. She still thought they would return on their own eventually.

Alice appeared on the bridge and called for them in the same way she always did, this time holding Adam in her mind. She would find him. She had all week.

Taking a seat on the ledge, she went over her notes. Adrianna had helped her with the pronunciation with a lot of new words when she wasn't with Wyatt, but they made her dizzy and lose focus whenever she tried to read them. Alice wondered why, but it was hard enough to get her focused on the words again that Alice hadn't asked more.

A loud crack from the woods made her look up. There were a few of Wonderland's people already walking out from the bushes to find her with hearts in their hands, these ones unattended. She knew one of them as the fox who had claimed to be her agent so many visits ago, but none of the rest were familiar. One of these days Adam or Matt would be the ones coming there, hopefully with their hearts still intact when they did so, and she could finally bring another brother back for Adrianna. For now, though, Wonderland had decided she had a job to do.

She smiled down at the four that walked toward her and she wondered how they kept finding her. It wasn't the bridge. While she liked coming to the bridge now, especially since it was so close to the White Rabbit's house, they found her in other areas. It was always when she was just sitting there, waiting for the brothers to come out. Alice wondered if somehow the spell was calling them out instead.

The hearts were only a little terrifying now. She was getting used to having them handed to her and she could return them two at a time now. They caught in her mind, this time the four creatures having switched them around in their hands, but Alice was able to set it right. The hearts knew where they belonged, and Alice set them all back in place.

"Why, hello Alice!" the Fox said. "What a pleasure to see you again! What brings you to these parts?"

"Returning your heart again," she said. "How do you keep getting it stolen? This is the second time I've had to put it back for you. You can't keep letting this happen, you know."

"Ah, well," he said, looking appropriately embarrassed. "There are some lovely eggs that the Queen of Hearts is attempting to keep for herself. It doesn't seem fair that she'd not let a poor fox like me take a few off her hands. If she didn't want them stolen, after all, she would not be putting them in a place that was so easy to take them from. I don't know why she's so upset whenever it happens."

"And where is she keeping them?" Alice asked, amused.

"Oh, right in the open. In a coop with only a few guards watching. And that awful dog, stupid thing. If she wanted no one to take them, she wouldn't be using that lazy dog to keep us hard working foxes out of there. It's really her own fault that this keeps happening. No reason to be taking my heart for *her* folly."

"Of course not," Alice said, rolling her eyes but keeping

the grin on her face. Of course he was stealing them from the Queen of Hearts. Where else would he be getting them from? And he had to blame her for his idea to steal them in the first place, because Wonderland had the logic of a snail shell, constantly looping around and around until it came back on itself. Or maybe that was the logic of a laptop cable mixed with headphone cords.

"Alice!" a voice came from above her. She looked up to find Peter swooping in and stopping in the air between her and the Fox.

"Excuse me!" the Fox said. "We were having a conversation!"

"So?" Peter asked, hanging upside down in the air and turning around to look at the Fox. "I want to talk to her now. Got a problem with that?" Peter dropped down from the air, brandishing his wooden sword. The Fox backed away and looked aghast at him.

"Well I never!" he said, taking his leave and muttering about how rude some people were. Alice watched him go. Peter didn't seem to think he'd done anything wrong as he put his sword back and he turned to her. He took a surprised step back when he saw Alice, her arms crossed and glaring at him.

"What's your problem?" he asked. "You seemed pretty happy about our adventure last time."

"You can't just pop in whenever you want and interrupt

what I'm doing," Alice told him. "Fox was right. You were being rude. You should apologize."

"To him?" Peter asked, incredulous. "But he's already gone. And it's in the past now. Let's go on another adventure!"

"I can't," Alice told him, checking her watch to see how much time had already passed with her waiting for one of them to show up. "I have to find Adam and Matt, and until I find them, I'm not going on any more adventures with you."

"But you can go on a couple," he said. "Come on, you gotta get away from being the hero of Wonderland for a little while and have some fun!"

Alice tensed up at the word. "I'm not the hero of anything," she said quickly, the sudden reminder of the Bandersnatch sending a chill through her. "I'm just looking for Adam and Matt. Once I find them, I'm done with this place."

"Even if there's still people walking around with their hearts in their hands?" Peter asked, eyebrows raised. "Even then, you're just going to leave Wonderland forever and hope it all fixes itself?"

"I call it the Peter Pan method."

"That's not fair. You don't know what it's like over there."

Alice shrugged, taking a step back and leaving her arms crossed as she looked at him. "You don't know what it used to be like here when the book was still around. It's creepy with all these people walking around with their hearts in their hands, but before they weren't around at all. And there was the book, with the thing that came out of it that took the hearts out. And that room. But it looks like someone else is dealing with it now," Alice said, waving at where the four of them had gone off down the road to.

"You can deal with the book in Neverland too," Peter suggested. "People tell me I should let someone else have some of the glory. I can't always be the hero, you know. It's tiring."

"Pass," Alice said. "I already had to deal with a dragon. I don't want to know what's in any of the other books after that. I kind of draw the line after one dragon."

"You have a *dragon*?" he asked, his eyes lighting up and flying several feet into the air. "That is so cool! Where is it? Do you still have it somewhere? We have to find the dragon!"

Alice shook her head. "I don't think so," she told him. "The Jabberwocky ran away from the Mad Hatter and now I have no idea where he's gotten to. And so long as he doesn't start eating hearts, I'm happy to leave him wherever he is. But it is a bit dangerous to have a random dragon just running around Wonderland..."

"Then we must vanquish it!" Peter said, taking his sword out and brandishing it against the sky. "Or I will. Girls just get captured whenever dragons are involved. But you can stay behind me when he attacks! I can protect you."

"He's going to set this on fire," Alice said, appearing in

front of him to push his sword back down to his side. "And then he'll set you on fire. He's probably just found a nice cave somewhere and he's going to hole up there for a while. Best to just leave him there until he starts causing more trouble."

"Cave?" Peter asked. "Which cave do you think he's in?"

"I don't know," Alice said. "One of them?"

"You don't know where the caves are in Wonderland, do you?" he asked. "You're supposed to be the hero of this place and you don't even know where the caves are!"

"I am not a hero!" Alice snapped at him. "I'm just a normal girl who keeps ending up here and is going to find Adrianna's brothers and then leave Wonderland forever and forget all about it. I'm not some hero that's going to save any- thing. I can't save anything."

"You saved one of the brothers, right?"

"I saved him because of the dragon," Alice told Peter. "I lured the dragon into the castle and got him out of there while everyone was distracted." It wasn't the whole truth, but Peter didn't need to know the rest. She neglected to mention that she was the distraction, not the dragon. She'd done none of the getting people out at all.

"Like that time I lured the crocodile in and right when Hook thought he had the upper hand—"

He stopped suddenly, his whole body falling into a slump as he seemed to remember something. His eyes clouded over and went dark as a memory gripped him and he fell back down to the ground, sitting there for a moment with his eyes staring off into the distance. "But he's gone now," he said. "He's gone and he's come back and he's gone. But he'll come back."

Alice didn't know what was going on, but she did feel a pang of sympathy for him. He reminded her of more than one occasion where she had sat there, trying desperately not to think about the hearts in that room beating all around her. She knelt down next to him, but he wouldn't stop staring into the distance. Words formed on his lips, but died before he could voice them.

"Do you want to go find the Jabberwocky?" Alice offered. "That's what the dragon is called. The Jabberwocky." It couldn't possibly take that long to find, and she had a week to look for Adam and Matt. Besides, she found a sign of Adam in a place she'd never been before. Maybe there would be something in these caves that would lead her to another brother.

"Looking for a dragon?" Peter asked, his voice getting a little stronger and a little less like a small, lost child. He blinked.

"Don't try to vanquish him," Alice said. "He won't like that much. But we can try to find it, at least. I can show you the last place I saw it. If you can keep up."

He laughed at that. "I'll call you when I get there first!" he said, zipping up off the ground and into the air. "Just listen for the crow!" He let out a bird call that did not sound like a crow at all. Alice waited on the ground, looking up with her arms crossed and a grin on her face, waiting for him to realize what he was missing.

He came back down a few minutes later. "Where did you say you saw it last?"

"I'll call you when I get there," she said, taking a step vanishing from her spot, appearing in the forest. "Keep up!"

Alice moved slowly through Wonderland so Peter could keep up. It was difficult for him to weave through the trees from the air, though he insisted on flying. Alice kept moving through the trees, vanishing with each step and appearing further ahead with the next, until they were in the middle of the forest.

"This is where I saw him last," Alice said, pointing at the tree that was still knocked over from when the Jabberwocky last made his escape. "When he was on the grounds at school, he found a nice cave to hide in. You know of a cave around here anywhere?"

Peter looked around on the ground for a moment before he shot up through the trees and into the sky. Alice watched him for a long moment before he came back down to get her.

Instead of answering her spread hands asking if he saw anything, he grabbed her by the wrists and lifted her up into the sky. She grabbed his wrists in return, panicking until they broke through the canopy of leaves where Alice could see the land around her. They weren't so far from a small hilly range, and a little beyond that was the plains where Tiger Lily and her tribe called home.

"You need to ask before you do that," Alice told him, though he didn't seem to care. She could at least see where the caves probably were. It wasn't that far, and she imagined that the Jabberwocky could have gotten into them somehow. But those weren't the only things that caught her attention from so high up.

She could see the sea from here. It lapped slowly along the shore, but there was something else that was off. There was hole in the ground near the hills that she could see going right through one of the small hills. It was dark on the other side, like the night that Wonderland never had, ominous and like something otherworldly was waiting, ready to sneak through. Alice didn't know what it was, but she had to see.

Alice let go of Peter's wrists. Peter hadn't been holding her that tightly and Alice dropped out of his hands, free falling straight down to the hole. Peter panicked as soon as she fell out of his hands, flying down to catch her again, but she was already gone.

She landed neatly at the top of the hill with more ease than she knew she should have. Her attention, though, was on the tear in the universe that was Wonderland, and everything around it. Now that she was here, she could see that hole wasn't the strangest thing. It was what the hole had been punched into.

From above and far away, it looked like the hills rolled out to the shore, but that was not the case here. Now that she was close, she could see a heavy sheet gently waving in the absence of a breeze that allowed the hills and ocean to show through it. It was like a theatre set that she could only see when she was up close, and she looked around to see where the rest of the edges were. It receded back out to the shore on either side, but it had come inland here, where something had made the hole.

Her hand was up and reaching out to touch it before she made the decision to do it. Slowly, she came forward, ready to snap her fingers back or run if it did anything more threatening than gently shift back and forth. She wondered if it was even real, or if she'd somehow found the very edge of the world. She wondered if it would move if she touched it. She wondered, and she was so close to knowing for sure.

"No!" Peter yelled at her, finally having reached her from way up in the sky.

It was too late. Her hand made contact with it and it felt like nothing under her fingers. A moment later, Alice realized that it was not a thing that could be felt like that.

She felt it inside her head, like something poured over her brain, then dripping down to coat even more underneath.

It was slimy and there were parts it didn't cover. There were holes pierced through the coating that stung like daggers, left open for horrible things to get in. She could feel points inside her brain as well where little pins pinched at the soft matter. And there was one large hole, one where her spine connected to her skull, that was left open and aching.

She didn't realize that she'd closed her eyes until she felt Peter's hands on her shoulders trying to shake her awake. She could hear him in the distance, slowly getting closer as the feeling of her coated brain being attacked started to fade away.

"Not you too. Come on, wake up!"

He had his hand raised and ready to slap her when she opened her eyes. "That was weird," she said, pushing herself up until she was sitting. She held her head as it started to finally clear. She could still feel those little holes in her brain, the dull stinging sensations that didn't want to go away. At least it was getting better. "How long was I out?"

Peter hugged her tight. He caught himself quickly and jumped away. "You can't do that!" he told her, not looking at her and blushing furiously. "Bad things happen when you touch the nothing."

"It's not really called the nothing," Alice said. Something so huge and encompassing that felt so powerful couldn't have such a stupid name. "There has to be a better name for it than that."

"Well what would *you* call it?"

Alice shook her head and ignored him for now, going back to the small hole in the sheet at the top of the hill. It was more like a crack, looking bigger and smaller as the sheet shifted, though it wasn't very large at all. And it was so dark over there, like it never was here. She reached her hand forward, but this time Peter grabbed her before she touched anything, taking her by the wrist and hoisting her away from the hole. "Don't touch it *again*!"

"But it's night on the other side," Alice said. "It's never night in Wonderland."

"It's weird," Peter agreed. "When does anyone sleep?"

"Why sleep when there's so much to do? Any more than a nap and you might as well be dead for all that life you've wasted dreaming." Alice stopped, realizing what she was saying. "Sorry, I don't know what that was," she said, her face puzzled as she tried to shake the cobwebs out of her mind.

"You're weird."

"If it's never night here, then it must be a land of nevers on the other side," Alice reasoned. "Is that Neverland on the other side? It doesn't look so bad over there. Kind of pretty. I wonder what kind of crumpets they have with tea over there."

"Alice?"

"Come along!" Alice said, smiling brightly and making her way down over the hill and away from the crack in the world.

She was feeling quite chipper all of a sudden. Full of curiosity and adventure. Somewhere in her, she knew this was odd, but there was something over there and she couldn't remember the last time she had seen something so strange. "We were looking for a dragon! Oh, I hope he has tea. I'm feeling a little peckish."

"Alice where are you — Wait!"

Alice wandered down the hill and found a small cave fairly quickly, possibly because of all of the disappearing and reappearing with every step. It was just easier to be where she wanted to go than actually walking all the way there, you see. Peter seemed to be having trouble keeping up, but Alice didn't know why he was complaining. He could surely do the same thing.

"This is a rather nice cave," Alice said as she stood at the entrance, looking inside. "A little dark, though."

"It's a cave," Peter told her. "Caves are dark."

"They could put in a window," Alice said, looking around it as she went in. "It looks like they have plenty of glass already. All they need now is to cut out a hole and it could be bright as day in here! Oh, why does this all seem so familiar? I feel like I've seen this before."

"Alice snap out of it," Peter told her, grabbing her by the shoulders and spinning her around.

Alice stepped out of his grasp and shook her head. "Has

no one ever taught you not to grab a lady?" she demanded. "Who taught you your manners?"

"You're acting really weird."

"And you're behaving quite rudely." She turned back around, walking into the rest of the cave and making comments on the lack of light as they went further and further into the dark. "I do wonder, can you hear that hissing sound? Very unpleasant."

Alice reached into her bag and pulled out the flashlight she'd left in there since the first time she went through the forest looking for the Jabberwocky. She turned it on and immediately found a black hide of scales. She kept creeping the light up and eventually found the eyes and the sideways snout. The Jabberwocky let out a roar and a stream of fire at the two of them.

"I think I've found the Jabberwocky! Terribly predictable place to be hiding, though."

Peter dived and knocked Alice to the ground, covering her before she could be hit with the flame. The flashlight fell out of her hand. It skittered away, but still shone its light on the Jabberwocky, who was pacing back and forth and drawing closer.

"He seems to be in a bit of a sour mood, though. I doubt he'll invite us to sit for tea."

"Alice, what is wrong with you?"

"I think the larger issue here is what is wrong with him," Alice said, nodding at the approaching Jabberwocky. Peter got up and picked Alice up with him, flying them both out of the way as the Jabberwocky swiped at them and tried to cook them alive. "He seems quite poorly behaved," she continued. "Not even a proper greeting or invitation, and after I was so good as to bring a little light to this dreary cave. One would expect a little gratitude."

"I don't think he likes you very much."

Peter dropped her on a small ledge out of the Jabberwocky's reach and perched next to her to watch the beast below as it tried to claw its way up. They were high enough that the Jabberwocky couldn't reach them, the cave too small for him to spread his wings and get out. He still took up the majority of the floor below them and completely blocked their only way out.

"I am still a guest," Alice said, clearly annoyed. "It is all fine and well to dislike a person, but this is not the appropriate treatment of a guest to one's own home."

Alice got to her feet and stared down hard at the Jabberwocky. He was clawing up the wall, hissing and growling and making no progress to get any closer to them. He pounded so hard on the wall that a crack appeared, showing a land of night on the other side of it.

Alice was far too annoyed by the Jabberwocky's behaviour

to realize the strangeness of that sheet extending down into the cave. Right now, it was a convenient door. "That's it," Alice snapped. "I will not be treated in this way. We are leaving."

Peter looked like he might have asked what her plan was, but she grabbed him by the wrist and pulled him towards the crack in the wall. It was just big enough for her and Peter and she stormed through it, furious at her treatment in the cave. She'd been knocked over, had that creature breathe fire at her, and still not so much as a hello! It was like he didn't even want them there!

"The nerve of the Jabberwocky!" she complained, dragging Peter with her into the dark land beyond the sheet. The foliage here was thick and it made it hard for her to continue storming away, but she was determined. "Why, I was only hoping to help! Putting in a mirror before you cut a hole for the window is definitely poor building practice. I may not have much practice in it myself, but it seems to me it's common sense!"

Peter protested at the end of her arm, but couldn't pull out of her grasp. He dug his heels in and tried to wrestle his hand free of her, but she continued to drag him onward. "We can't be here!" he said. "We have to go back! Dragons are better than being back here!"

"Dragons are rude an— Peter?" she asked suddenly, her grip on his wrist loosening as she did so. "I'm very tired."

Alice felt herself fall backwards, but didn't remember hitting the ground before she was fast asleep.

CHAPTER 13

Alice in Neverland

ALICE WAS PRETTY sure she was at the bottom of a hole when she woke up. The sun was just breaking through the trees above her. The canopy of the trees was up much farther than it should have been. There was dirt on either side, cut into very nice, clean walls. She was lying on a bed of grass and branches, none of which was very comfortable. Her wrist ached.

She sat up and her head started spinning. She let out a groan and cupped her face in her hands, waiting for the spinning to finally come to a halt.

"This is your fault, you know," Peter said, sitting in a corner with his knees up to his chest. "I didn't want to come back here, but then *you went crazy! What happened to you?*"

"Don't shout," Alice groaned, grabbing her pounding head and trying to block out the noise of him. "I have the worst headache. And I seem to have woken up in a hole. Why are we in a hole?"

Alice went to the backpack still on her back and pulled out a bottle of water. She couldn't trust any of the food or drink in Wonderland, after all, so she came prepared with a few snacks and water for when she got hungry. Thankfully, they seem to have survived the fall and she pulled out a couple snacks. "Chocolate bar?" she offered Peter.

"Are you still crazy?" he asked, looking suspiciously between the chocolate and her.

"I'm sorry about that," Alice said, smiling apologetically as he took the chocolate. "I don't really know what happened. Was I really mad at the Jabberwocky about interior decorating?"

"And because it was dark in a cave."

Alice let out an embarrassed laugh. "Can we just never talk about that ever again?" She didn't want to think about what had happened back there because she didn't understand what happened to her. It all made sense at the time.

Peter sat there, eating the chocolate bar and staring at her without saying anything. Alice didn't know what else to do about it, so she ate and drank and tried to get up. A spasm shot through her leg from her knee, dull but enough that she knew that she had done something to it. She could bend it a little before the pain came, but she wasn't going to be able to do much moving.

Then she realized. They were in the bottom of a hole and Peter could not only fly, but he regularly picked her up and flew her out of places without asking her first. While she would understand if he decided to leave her there, she didn't know why he was still down here with her.

"What?" he asked, shrinking back from the way she stared at him.

"Why didn't you fly out?" she asked.

"I wasn't going to leave you here," he said. "You might be crazy, but you're still a girl. You need to protect girls."

"You could have flown me out too," Alice said.

"But you were sleeping."

"You can't fly, can you?"

"I can!"

"Prove it."

Peter curled up behind his legs and looked away, refusing to answer her. So that wasn't the way to get out of here. She would have to have to figure out how to get herself out of this.

She let out a dramatic sigh and got to her feet, wincing and trying not to put any weight on her bad knee. It wasn't too bad, so long as she didn't put too much weight on it. She limped forward a step and appeared at the top of the hole.

When Peter didn't follow, she started limping around to try and find a rope to throw down.

"What are you doing?" Peter called up to her. "Where did you go?"

"I'm just looking for a rope," she said, finding a vine that looked thick enough to hold his weight and tried to pull it down off the tree. It was tough with her leg, but she grabbed it and gave it a tug before she went off balance and fell backwards. That was enough for her to pull it free. "If you aren't flying out, then you're going to have to get out some other way, right?"

"I can get out on my own!" he said.

"Then bring my backpack up with you and let's go," Alice said, bringing the rope over and throwing it down. She tied it around a stump and smiled down at him, taking a seat on the edge of the hole and waiting for him to climb back up. "Come on. You said it was dangerous out here, right? We should get going."

A howl broke through the tension and they both looked up. The bright daylight had actually brought the wolves out, it seemed. The howl sounded off, though Alice could not quite place why it sounded so strange. It was just off, wrong somehow and very much distorted in a way that Alice couldn't place.

Peter below her froze. "You should get back in here," he said.

"What are they going to do, talk me to death?"

"They aren't Wonderland wolves, Alice. Neverland wolves are actually going to try and eat you!"

Alice rolled her eyes and reached to the side, putting her arm in the ground. The backpack down below shuffled, making Peter jump, and she got out her notebook, looking through the section on spells. She knew she had something prepared for if the Jabberwocky attacked that she wanted to try, but she could always replace it with wolves.

"You're sure they're wolves?" she asked, flipping through the book. "Not something else?"

"What are you doing? They are going to eat you!"

Alice ignored him, finding the right words as she went through the book. She was less panicked than she should be and still found Peter to be a bit more rude than necessary, which made her think that maybe she hadn't completely shaken off whatever the nothing had done to her. Mentally, she kicked herself for using that stupid term for it and continued looking for what she needed.

Peter kept hissing to try and convince her to get down there with him where they might be able to hide, but she shook her head, not looking up from the book. She knew it was written in here somewhere. "They'll find us and then just jump in the hole with us," Alice told him. "And you can't fly out. Trust me, we'll be fine. Just give me a minute."

"You're nuts!" he snapped at her. "They're going to eat you! At least hide or something!"

Something came out of the bushes and Alice half expected it to be a wolf in a waistcoat holding his heart. Instead, it was a small stream of wolves, all looking like they hadn't eaten in quite a while. They were missing patches of fur and both looked and smelled like they were rotting away. They bared their teeth and growled at her, looking like they were ready to kill if she made any move at all. They would probably kill if she didn't move as well.

Her first thought was that it was awful rude of them to interrupt without an introduction. She was going to have to break herself of whatever the nothing had done, because she was thinking too much like she was from Wonderland and it was definitely going to get her in trouble. She was staring down zombie wolves and not panicking, instead worrying about their manners.

"Are those wolves dead?" Alice asked, looking back down at her book. On the other hand, she was a lot calmer in this situation than she had any right to be. "Hang on, I got this."

"*Run!*" Peter snapped at her.

That was enough to get the wolves to start moving, but as the first one pounced, Alice got to her feet several feet away from them. She left the book on the stump for now. "*Áblinnan hold mammilia carnivora caniformia canidae hámsíþ.*" Her hands moved from up above her head and spread outwards, her mind conjuring the image of a den that the wolves called their temporary home, filled with bones and other wolves that were now too decayed to continue hunting. They reconnected in the right direction of where that cave was. She flicked her wrists upwards and threw her hands in the direction that they were supposed to go, ignoring the flicker of pain that went through her wrist.

The wolves stopped, staring at her. A moment later, they all filed out. One by one, they glared at her and left through the same bushes they had entered through.

"That was easy," Alice said. "And probably a lot more terrifying than I'm currently giving it credit for. You can come up now."

"What did you do?" Peter asked, not even remotely trusting the rope. "You just said a bunch of gibberish!"

"Didn't Tiger Lily tell you?" Alice asked a little too calmly. "She kidnapped me and kept me in a tent all drugged up because I am a witch. I can do super witchy things. Like tell wolves to go back home. Those were dead wolves, right? I'm pretty sure those wolves were dead."

"You're not like any witch I ever met," Peter said, finally climbing up the rope and leaving her backpack on the ground below. Alice rolled her eyes, resisting the urge to tell him how rude he was, and picking it up herself.

"Because I'm not an ugly hag?" Alice asked as she shrugged the backpack onto her back, shoving her notebook back into it. She remembered that much from when Tiger Lily had teased her. "I really think you should think about flying again. Why can't you fly here? You fly in Wonderland. Did you eat something that let you fly over there? You ate something, didn't you?"

"I learned to fly from the birds!" he told her. "I can still fly! I just don't want to right now." He started to walk on through the forest without her and Alice hobbled along after him, going slowly and finding her leg throbbed more the more she walked. She tried desperately not to let out any sounds of pain, but it was still on her face when he looked back. "What's wrong with you?"

"I did something to my knee when I fell," Alice told him. "Can you slow down a little?"

Peter came back beside her and put her arm around his shoulders. He was a little short, but just right for Alice to lean on, and they kept walking.

"Thanks," Alice said. Peter didn't say anything, instead looking wildly around at the forest for any movement in the trees. Alice wasn't sure what was going on, but he was definitely starting to make her paranoid.

"What are you looking for?" she asked. "More dead things going to come up from nowhere and attack us again?"

"Yes," he said. "We're not in nice fun Wonderland anymore. We weren't supposed to come back here. I just wanted to fight a dragon, not come back here."

"It doesn't seem so bad. Well, except for the rotting wolves that came after us, but we were stuck in a hole for… How long were we stuck in that hole for? It was night when we came through and it's daytime now, so…"

Alice looked at her watch, finding that a day had passed. Strangely, the seconds hand was working, unlike in Wonderland where the watch face was frozen when she watched. Time in Neverland, apparently, worked different. It was a place where night existed, which still seemed strange to her.

"We need to get out of here," he said.

"What happened?" she asked. "I told you what happened in Wonderland. The book and the Queen of Hearts and the hearts being taken out of everyone. And you've seen how everyone is just kind of walking around holding their hearts now. You know all about Wonderland and the book there, but now that I'm here, I know nothing about Neverland. And you wanted me to save this place."

"You *are* going to save this place," Peter said. "You'll save it and I'll let someone else do it for once. I'm so tired of always saving everyone on my own all the time. It's time someone else saved the day for once. So people can see how much better I am at doing it."

"Yeah, sure," Alice said, not really paying as much attention to the manic tone that seeped into his words. "You do that. So what happened? There was a book?"

"The black book," he said, Alice hearing as his voice hooked into some dark memory that he was only barely ready to recall now. "It's the pirates' fault. They kidnapped her and gave her that book. And then the pirates were gone and she had the book, but she didn't want to be our mother anymore. She got mad whenever anyone tried to ask for a story or to get something sewn or anything."

His eyes focused on the very far distance and Alice tried to make sure they didn't bang into any trees as they walked. It was easy enough, Peter being so light he was easy to steer, but she didn't know where they were going. After a moment, he came back to himself, his steps turning off into a smaller path from the main one that was harder for Alice to walk through.

"So this woman," Alice said. "She had the black book and started doing bad things with it. And now there's dead wolves wandering around and smelling terrible all over the place? That sounds pretty bad. Have you tried getting the book away from her? Maybe talking to her? Making her understand that the things she is doing are wrong and hurting people?"

"She won't listen," Peter said. "I don't think she can hear anyone anymore. Everyone who went to try to talk to her never came back. Or they did and that was worse. It was better when they never came back. A lot of the Lost Boys died. And not in the usual way. Usually, when a Lost Boy dies, he just gets too old and he goes home after we kill him in one last game. What she does isn't a game."

"I'm sorry, the lost boys?" Alice asked. "There's a whole group of you lost kids just living out here on your own? Where are your parents?"

"We don't need parents!" Peter said, some of his confidence coming back. "We are the Lost Boys and we can handle anything. We live for adventure and battle pirates and find treasure and explore far off lands. We can do whatever we want without parents."

"Except for that mother person of yours," Alice said. "Until she found the book. You know, I think you need to go back a little. I'm getting a bit lost in all this. So there's a bunch of lost kids in the woods and there's one woman who takes care of all of you and just lets you go out and run around in… that," Alice said, taking another look over Peter's complete patchwork of clothing that he insisted on wearing that, as far as she was aware, did not consist of pants. "What about girls? Are there any lost girls?"

"No," Peter said. "There was one Lost Girl. She was our mother. I brought her back to read stories to us and tuck us into bed and be our mother. She brought her brothers with her to be Lost Boys. But I don't think she liked being a Lost

Boy that much. And then the black book happened and it all got so much worse."

"So you kidnap people?" Alice asked. This whole thing was getting confusing, but also parts of things were making sense. At the very least, she knew why he kept lifting her up from the ground and dragging her to places whether she wanted to go or not. "Where did any of these people come from? Did you kidnap these lost boys too, or did they just wander in here on their own?"

"It's not like that," Peter said, though he looked like he didn't really know how to defend himself, nor that he wanted to. "They said they wanted to come and Tink just sprinkled them with fairy dust. We taught them to fly and they came on their own."

"Tink?"

"Tinkerbelle," Peter said. "We're going to try and find her. You're no good if I gotta carry you everywhere."

"Unless you get more dead wolves," Alice said. "Then I'm really useful." The effects of the nothing were wearing off now and, though she joked, she was starting to realize that she had been looking at rotting corpses that were trying to eat her. While being able to focus on their rudeness and the stench they gave off was helpful, she knew she hadn't felt quite the fear or gravity of the situation at the time. She needed to stay focused.

That feeling on her brain wasn't quite completely gone yet. She still had some of it, like her brain was covered in icing and stabbed with knives. It was an unsettling feeling that she was unable to shake and she knew it wouldn't go away anytime soon. The best she could do for now was hope it wouldn't affect too much.

"Tell me about Tinkerbelle," Alice said, hoping to keep Peter talking about things that didn't make him stare off into the distance and would distract her from how much her leg hurt. The more he talked, the less she had to pay attention to the silence around them, an unnatural quiet for the forest, and the inability she had to walk properly.

"She's a fairy," he said. "She doesn't say much sometimes and sometimes she really doesn't know when to stop talking. She's one of my best friends and she comes with me wherever I go. Or she used to. She went off to talk to the other fairies before I went off to Wonderland and I haven't seen her in a while. But I'm sure she's at the fairy village with the other fairies."

"Fairies?" Alice asked. This place that was supposed to be so dangerous and so scary and that's what they had? "There's fairies here?"

"Yeah," Peter said as if it were the most natural thing in the world. "Fairies and mermaids. But they're all girls, so they don't really like adventure too much. And they don't really like each other too much either, so you have to keep them apart or they fight. Why do girls always fight with each other?"

"We don't," Alice said. "My best friends are girls. And boys. Maybe you just hang out with weird girls."

Peter shrugged. The forest was getting thicker now and Alice knew they were getting close to something. He kept making weird turns into thicker and thicker parts of the forest, but he was taller now. He walked, but Alice could see his feet were no longer on the ground. He was calm and the talking seemed to be helping keep him from thinking of the scary stuff that was keeping him on the ground.

"So how do you fly, exactly?" Alice decided to ask. Best not to ask about the kidnapping, though she wanted to know about that too. "You said something about fairy dust and birds?"

"The birds taught me," Peter said. "And then I met the Fairy Queen and she said I could fly whenever I wanted. Or was that the other way around? Either way, I could always do it, but with the Lost Boys, it's a little different. They *have* to use fairy dust to fly. With that, you get a little dust on you, and then you just have to think of a happy thought. Any happy thought. The happiest one you can think of. And when you can think of it, then you can fly! It's easy. And that's what you're going to do."

"Why do I need to fly?" Alice asked. Not that she was

opposed to flying, but she didn't see why she'd need to. "We aren't staying in Neverland. I thought we might just check in on the fairies and then head back to Wonderland. We aren't going back to Wonderland?"

"Not yet," Peter said, suddenly very determined about this whole thing. "First, you're going to save Neverland. And then I'll take you back to Wonderland."

"I'm not saving Neverland," Alice said. "I never said I was saving Neverland."

"But you already saved Wonderland," Peter said, grabbing onto Alice's arm harder when she tried to pull away. For someone so small and light, he was a lot stronger when he was in the air.

"I didn't agree to this," she told him. "I didn't agree to any of this. You're the one who wanted to save Neverland. You're the hero, right? Why don't you do it? Just steal the book and tell this mother lost girl, or whatever she is, to get a hold on herself and stop doing whatever it is she's doing. Bringing the dead back or whatever. What do you need me for?"

"You already saved Wonderland," he repeated. "If you saved Wonderland, you'll save Neverland. I'll even tell people you did it so they'll believe you did it. I let you save it instead. Yes, that's what's happened. And then they will be nice to you. And you can be our new mother instead and it will all go back to the way it was."

"I am not going to be your mother," Alice said. "That's never happening."

"Back to the way it was before," Peter muttered. "And then Hook will come back. And I'll find some new Lost Boys. Better Lost Boys. And we'll all go off and have adventures and you'll tell us we need to clean and fix our clothes and read us stories and it will all go back to normal."

"I can see why this girl didn't like you much," Alice muttered. If not for her leg and the grip he had on her arm, she would be gone. Even with all that, she was having trouble moving anywhere on her own. She didn't know this place and had nowhere to go. She didn't really remember the place where she'd come out of Wonderland and had no idea how to get back there now.

"Oh, we're almost there!" Peter said. His eyes lit up, but Alice didn't see why. She could see the thing in the distance as well and she knew this was going to go poorly. There was a veil of willow leaves that hid away something that was clearly there, but it was tattered. She could see through the cracks in the leaves that something had been there. Things looked destroyed in the silhouette of that veil, though Peter didn't notice.

He dragged her, faster now, which made her wince. She didn't bother hiding her pain anymore, letting out a few yelps as she was forced to put more weight on that leg than she wanted to. It wasn't going to support her at all and Peter was probably making it worse.

Peter let her go and she dropped to the ground. She didn't bother stopping him as he reached forward and separated the willow veil, watching as his face dropped.

There was only destruction. It looked like it had been burned down long ago, the carved wooden houses that once stood there now white and black and looking like they would crumble if she touched anything. He walked to the center of it, looking around at the destruction with his eyes wide. He went to touch one house, watching it crumble under his hands. He stepped away from it, looking like he might cry. He was lost and went looking around, his flight returning so that he could peer around into every house, saying panicked things in a way that Alice could barely make out as he went through all of them.

Alice would feel sympathy for him if she wasn't sure that her leg wasn't completely screwed up now. Peter's dragging her around left her a little less than sympathetic. She watched as he flew back and forth and instead took more issue with the fact that there seemed to be a pair of eyes watching them from the other side of the willows.

"Peter?" the voice said from the other side of the leaves. "Peter Pan? Is that you?"

Peter jumped as a boy came into the ruined village, tall

and lanky and looking to be around fifteen years old. Alice didn't know who he was, but he seemed to know Peter and he hadn't seen Alice sitting there nursing her knee yet. Instead, he approached Peter with a childlike wonder in his eyes. His hero had returned.

"It *is* you!" he said. "You've come back to save us!"

"John!" Peter said. "You're so old. What happened?"

"He's, like, fifteen," Alice said, shaking her head and staring at them.

"Peter, who is she?" he asked.

"She is Alice," Alice said, trying and failing to stand. With the slightest weight on it, her knee crumbled under her and she stayed sitting. "Hi. I'm just being dragged along. Peter's gone nuts. Don't mind me."

"She's going to save Neverland," Peter said, looking almost proud of it. "I always save it. I don't want to this time, so she's going to do it."

"I didn't agree to that," Alice said.

"She's already saved a whole other world already."

"I did not actually save another world."

"She can disappear!"

"Not quite."

"Would you be quiet?" he snapped at her. "I'm trying to talk to John."

Alice smiled with her lips tight, hands up in surrender and looking around at the destroyed fairy village. She thought it was a little strange that someone would be able to burn down a village and fail to burn down the tree that hid it.

"Peter, you're not really going to make her do it?" John asked. His admiration and love of Peter seemed to turn to fear in that moment. "*You're* supposed to save it. You're supposed to save all of us. What about Wendy? Wendy will listen to you! You have to be the one to save her, Peter!"

"Yeah Peter," Alice said. "You have to save her. And with no fairies, it looks like I'm not going to be able to fly, so I can't do anything, right?"

"You'll still figure out something," Peter said. He was starting to sound a little crazy. "You already saved Wonderland. You can save Neverland too. And I can take a break just this one time and let someone else do it. None of the Lost Boys will do it."

"What?" John asked. "Peter, no, what's going on? Aren't you back to save us? After what happened to Hook—"

"No!" Peter said, turning on John. "Someone else this time! You're all always whining at me. Save us, Peter! You have to save us Peter! We've gotten ourselves in trouble again and kidnapped and we can't get out of it on our own, so *you* need to come to the rescue, Peter! Well, not this time! This time, I'm not going to save anyone and you're all going to have to do it all on your own and I won't help you! Not even a little! If you want help, you ask her!"

Peter took out his sword and swung it to point at Alice, who was no longer in the spot she'd been recovering. She left her backpack behind, but both of them looked around for her and found nothing.

"Yes, the backpack will save you," Alice said, sitting up in the branches of the willow and looking down. "It is a brave warrior, you know. It's done a great many deeds. Conquered all of the creatures that have ever opposed it. You will be in good hands, relying on the inanimate backpack to save you. Good thing I'm off the hook."

"How did you...?" John asked, Alice dropping out of the tree and vanishing behind the branches.

Alice appeared next to John, leaning on him for support against her busted knee and smiling at him with a pain riddled grimace. "Peter's gone crazy," she said to him simply. "I'm not saving you. He's not saving you. I'm actually probably going to start trying to get out of here. I saw a nice mirror over there. If you want, I'll bring you back with me to Wonderland. You seem like a nice crutch."

Peter hurled his wooden sword at the mirror that Alice had indicated, smashing it into a million tiny pieces. That bit of Wonderland in her brain was taking over pretty thoroughly now and she let herself give into it. She was tired, in pain and didn't want to deal with this anymore.

"Well that was rude," Alice said. "Where are your manners?"

"You will save Neverland."

"No," Alice said. "I don't think I will. I think John agrees. If anyone should be saving the land that you're the hero of, it should be you. This Wendy girl, it sounds like you and her have a few unresolved issues. You should probably talk to her. Open communication is the basis for a good solid relationship. Honesty and all that."

Alice smiled as he took another swing at her, going to sit by her backpack again. She picked it up and looked through it. "I really need to pack a first aid kit in this thing," Alice said. "It seems so obvious now that I need one. Not that it will help. John, do you know how to splint a knee? I don't know if I've broken it or what, but I'm pretty sure it needs some sort of splint."

She looked between the two of them for a moment and noticed Peter had picked up that deranged look in his eyes again. John reached forward to hold him back, but Peter leapt at Alice as she leaned back and disappeared into the ground.

She appeared not far away on the trail and tried to get back to her feet soundlessly. She heard Peter crash through the willow on the other side. She looked forward and took a few steps, disappearing and reappearing as far away as she could manage each time, which was not as far as she could travel in Wonderland. She didn't know what else to do but get away from Peter.

The pain in her leg was getting to be too much. She had to stop, collapsing against a tree to catch her breath and trying to keep it from throbbing. She needed to get away from here, find a mirror and get back to Wonderland. If she could get to Wonderland from here in the first place. She had no idea what she could and could not do, and the pain was making it hard for her to concentrate.

There was something walking in the forest. It came from her left and she didn't want to encounter it. Best case, it was a wolf and she already knew how to get rid of it. Worst, it was Peter and he was going to try and make her save Neverland again.

Or it could be something else shambling towards her. There was a pirate coming forward on a peg leg, walking slowly and deliberately. He was missing his lower jaw and had been dead for quite a while from the smell of him.

Alice needed to go.

She got up, resisting the urge to let her leg collapse under her and steeling herself against the pain. She found herself no faster than the pirate in her condition, having to take a break against each tree he came closer to until she finally looked back. There was a rustle from above and she looked up.

A dark figure dropped out of the trees, landing on the dead man and slicing off his head. He dropped lifeless onto the ground and the woman with the knives turned. Alice's heart leapt into her throat as she recognized Tiger Lily now looking at her and drawing closer. Alice tried to scramble away, but she lost her balance and fell to the ground.

"I wish you no harm, Alice of Wonderland," Tiger Lily said. "Peter Pan seeks you and this place is dangerous. I wish to bring you back to Wonderland."

"Why?"

"We have much to discuss, Alice of Wonderland," Tiger Lily said. "Consider this the first part of a long apology." Tiger Lily extended a hand down to Alice.

Alice looked at it for only a moment before she heard that crow of Peter's. She took Tiger Lily's hand and let her carry her through the forest.

CHAPTER 14

Apologies and a Gift

TIGER LILY ENDED up carrying Alice on her back through the tear, Alice unable to walk anymore. They didn't have time to splint it, Peter catching up on the trail and convincing John that Alice was a witch that they would use in a plan to take down Wendy. The two of them flew overhead and, with Alice on her back, Tiger Lily had to weave through the forest, hiding at every moment to try and keep out of sight.

Alice did what she could to help. After the first time, Alice dropped off her back to hide under a bush, Tiger Lily started pointing out places for her to hide from the boys while she did the same, then Alice would appear on her back when she showed herself again and they would be on their way.

She stopped at the crack in the universe that led to Wonderland. There was a cave on the other side, Alice knew, dark and unnerving. Tiger Lily looked longingly up at the top of the tear, then back down to the base where they would have to pass through instead.

"There is a great dragon on the other side," Tiger Lily said. "He is most ferocious."

"I got this one," Alice said. She was getting tired. It was getting late and the sun was retreating from the sky. Alice was hungry, though they could not stop to eat with the boys chasing after them. Time had passed while they were in Neverland in a way that was very different than what she was used to in Wonderland and she just wanted to go home.

Alice reached into her bag and pulled out her book, smiling at Tiger Lily and nodding. "Trust me, I know what I'm doing."

"You had better, Alice of Wonderland," Tiger Lily said. Alice flipped the book open to her notes as Tiger Lily took them both through.

It felt like a knife in Alice's brain twisted as they went through. That feeling of something coating the inside of her head was still there and their passage felt like an extra tear running through it into her exposed brain tissue. She twitched and Tiger Lily slowed when Alice slumped on her back. Alice managed to straighten up as they made it through, urging her to continue.

The Jabberwocky wasted no time pouncing on them,

Tiger Lily dodging to the side as Alice vanished off her back and back up to the ledge where she had crossed over before. She flipped through, found the page, and reminded herself of the spell that was there.

"Haste, Alice of Wonderland!" Tiger Lily called up to her. "You would not leave me here after all I have done for you!"

"Done *to* me, too," Alice added quietly, but she was back down on the ground a moment later, balancing on one leg and her hands ready to do what they needed to do. She cleared her mind to prepare for the spell.

"*Ábedecian ásric ælwih Jabberwocky álætan*" she said, pushing the air back and down in front of her towards the Jabberwocky. The Jabberwocky resisted her urgings and Alice was having trouble keeping it together. Her leg hurt and she was going to fall, distracting her from what she was doing. Tiger Lily came up behind her, holding her up and Alice made an extra push, forcing her hands down against an invisible wall.

The Jabberwocky lay down on the spot, finally giving in. He went to sleep on the ground, Alice feeling her strength drain from her and crumpling into a heap in Tiger Lily's arms. It was already a long day and she had done so much. Her leg hurt, her arm hurt, and she could feel the watch continue to scratch the inside of her wrist, telling her none of this was a dream. It pushed a little harder now, her wrist swollen and Alice wanting nothing more than to sleep.

THIS TIME, THE teepee smelled sweet when Alice woke up. Her mind felt a lot clearer, though there was still the dull ache where she could feel the hole to Neverland. Alice wondered if that was actually the edges of Wonderland that she was feeling.

She was lying on a bed on the floor. Her wrist and her leg were covered now in leaves and cloth, wrapped tightly and splinted. They didn't hurt as badly and she could tell the swelling had gone down. Above her, there was no pot of incense that smelled like nothing crushing her. Tiger Lily sat on the other side of the tent, poring over something that Alice could not see.

Alice tried to sit up, but the action made her cough and brought the attention of Tiger Lily. She came over with a glass of water and offered it to her. Alice took it herself rather than letting Tiger Lily feed it to her and drank. She hoped it was safe, but at the moment, there wasn't much Alice could do about it. She didn't appear to be growing or shrinking or changing forms, and her mind still seemed about as together as it once was.

"Thank you, "Alice said, looking suspiciously at Tiger Lily. "You aren't going to try to drug me and keep me here again, are you?"

"Words are not apology enough for what I have done," she said. "I have a great repentance to make to too many people."

"Did you kidnap and drug more people than just me?" Alice asked. "I really hope that's not becoming a habit, Tiger Lily. People really don't like being kidnapped and drugged."

Tiger Lily looked defeated as she sat before Alice. "It was my father's wish. It was mine at first. We would use your magic to bring food and healing back to our tribe. We were suffering and desperate. I told my father what I had seen you do and what you had told me. I am ashamed to admit it was my idea to capture you and make you learn to return the hearts. It was my plan to sell you so that our tribe might eat."

"You know food grows on trees here now, right? Like, they grow fridges that are fully stocked. Meat and everything. And I think I told you that if you don't think about it, you just never get hungry in the first place."

"I would have done well to listen," Tiger Lily said. "When you escaped us, my father was furious. I had asked that you be released. What we had done — what *I* had done — was cruel and not our way. He said I had released you and I was cast out until I could return you to them. It will be a very long time before I will ever obey that command," she added at the end, noting Alice's worried expression. "I disagree with my father and he is the Chief. If he has cast me out, so be it. I must accept his decision."

"I'm sorry," Alice said. "But thanks. For not taking me back there."

Tiger Lily turned and got something from where she was sitting before. "If you take this, no one will be able to trap you again," she said, handing Alice a book. It was covered in red leather. It was the same size as the brown book and it was warm when Alice took it, almost like it was alive. She stared down at it and rested it on her lap, still holding it in both hands. It felt just like the brown book. It could have been its twin, but in red.

"What is this?"

"It came to me," Tiger Lily said, looking Alice in the eye and looking sombre about it. "I did not know what it was. I could feel it was a powerful thing and I was foolish. I hid it away where no one would find it. Inside, there is a way to hold you in place. If you take this, no one else will be able to hold you again."

"Where did you get this?" Alice asked. "Did it fall from the sky for you too?"

Tiger Lily looked at her oddly. "It fell from the clouds to land at my feet. You have seen this before."

Alice shook her head. "That's how the Queen of Hearts found her book, though."

"The book is evil," Tiger Lily said. "I have only used it for horrible things. It is like the other one. It's sister, the black book, has destroyed Neverland. Its brother, you have told me what the brown one has done to Wonderland. These books are evil, but you have read the brown one without turning. You are special, Alice of Wonderland. I can trust this book with you and it will never be used against you."

Alice looked down at the book, feeling none of this evil that Tiger Lily spoke of. It felt powerful, sure, much like the brown book had. But she had learned that the book was less evil than the person wielding it. And there were still so many more questions that she wanted answers to.

"What happened in Neverland?" Alice asked. "What made it like that? There were dead wolves hunting and that dead man was walking in the woods. And Peter, was he always like that? How did that happen?"

"It is a long story, Alice of Wonderland."

"I have time," she said with a bit of a smile. She reached over to her backpack, her hand going in while the rest of her stayed seated, and she pulled out an apple and a banana. She offered Tiger Lily the apple. "I always bring these, but I don't really like apples that much."

Tiger Lily took it, seeming a bit relieved, and sat across from Alice on the bed to tell her story. She took a knife out and cut the apple for herself to eat as she spoke.

"There was a time that Neverland was at peace. As peaceful as Neverland could be. Peter Pan and his Lost Boys had gotten in trouble with the pirates again. This was normal. We Piccaninny do not trouble ourselves with their affairs until they trouble us. We did not realize what had happened or we may have done something.

"Peter Pan kept one girl in his tribe of boys. Wendy was expected to care for them. She was taken by the pirates. She has been taken many times before, but this time was different. When she was taken, she was permitted to read. They gave her a book that fell to the deck and she learned from it. It is told that when Peter Pan and his Lost Boys came to rescue her, there were no pirates left. They suspected nothing and she gave Peter Pan the sword of Captain James Hook."

Tiger Lily went slowly through the next part, thinking and trying to get her words and thoughts together. "She was brought back and unhappy with what she was asked. She chose not to take care of the boys any longer. When they demanded that she continue, she grabbed one. It has been told that she took her scissors and cut him open. She removed the parts she did not like, then she sewed him back together. He still moved, but you cannot live when you have had your stomach removed."

Tiger Lily left a beat to let that sink in. She held Alice's gaze and took a breath before she continued.

"It was not long before she would do this to all that got in her way. She left the trees where the boys lived and found another place to make her home. She stole it from wolves, but now they are loyal to her as well. Those who are sensible run. Only one ever tried to stay and stop her."

"Peter?" Alice asked, already seeing where this was going.

"Peter Pan does not say much about what happened. He spoke of blood when I found him. Blood does not scare those who hunt, but he is a boy. He did not understand what death was. He spoke of one of the boys as if he had become pieces of a boy. Like the wolves had torn him, but it was Wendy instead. He spoke nonsense, but I have brought this much sense to it.

"He would not be left alone. He followed me as I hunted. I attempted to get away. He wished to play, to pretend it had never happened. He demanded an adventure and he brought me with him whether I chose it or not. He wished to run and he wished a companion to run with. This was how we came to the place at the edge of the world.

"My people always knew of this place. Deep in the forest, there is a place where you can go no farther. You walk into it and you come back out. For my people, we call it the T'éel Çanuu at times. It is like a tarp to cover the next world where we must not pass. We go there as a rite of passage when we come of age. It is a way for our people to understand that the world has been made vast, but there will always be secrets and there will always be an end to it."

She shook her head and tried to piece everything together of what happened next. Alice watched her, quietly finishing the banana and flexing her wrist beneath the leaves. It felt better, like it was completely healed. She wondered how long she'd been sleeping there, but she could ask when the story was done.

"Peter Pan brought me there. It was before I was meant to, but I was excited. I did not know what was going to happen. Peter Pan told me what had happened as we went and I took it for one of his stories. I should have known it was not. He was not himself when he told it, but I worried that he would not take me. I did not realize.

"When we got there, I tried to touch the edge. I could feel it, but still walked into it. It was not solid. Not for me. I walked into it for a few steps and it sent me back. It was strange.

"Peter was different. He did not pass through. He touched it and was strange afterwards. It became solid when he touched it and something happened to him that I do not understand. He yelled about adventure on the other side. He took the pirate captain's sword and began to attack the T'éel Çanuu. He was laughing, happy and playful and it was like he was attacking the pirates once more. He stuck the sword in and ran it right down, creating the tear. Where I could not touch it, he had cut it open and created a world.

"He left me there. I would not pass through. I was not even meant to be there yet and my tribe would be furious that I had gone to the edge before my time, so I had to find my own way back. My people lived so far from there. It took me days to find my way, but when I did, I wished I had gone with him.

"I was too late to save my tribe. I returned to find that Wendy had come with her book. She wished to take our warriors and our women to tend to her. She claimed some and threatened to take more. My people fought back. It was a mistake. Our village was set on fire and we left with what little remained. I led them to the tear at the end of the world and my father led us through to this land."

"I'm sorry you had to go through all of that," Alice said. "And now you can't even go back because of me."

"My father is blinded by the love of his people," Tiger Lily told her. "We have suffered greatly. I will be accepted back one day when I have proven myself. I have already found a guide who will lead me through Wonderland and teach me its ways so that I may learn skills to bring back to my tribe."

"A guide?"

"He has guided me to you," she said. "He showed me where you had gone and told me that I would get a chance to redeem myself if I returned you. The first of many wrongs would be made right. He told me that you would accept the book."

"Who?" Alice asked.

"He is called the Cheshire Cat," Tiger Lily said.

"Of course it's the Cheshire Cat," Alice said, rolling her eyes. "Tiger Lily, be careful with him. He speaks in riddles and, though he never quite lies, he also never really tells the truth either. He's a dangerous ally to have. That dragon in the cave? I said the words to let it out, but the Cheshire Cat is the one that held me down and made me read it."

"Perhaps he is also trying to make amends."

"Perhaps he is trying to convince me to let him back through into my world again so that he can escape the Queen of Hearts. She really wants his heart on a stick for some reason. Granted, she's never liked him, but he seems pretty adamant about getting out of Wonderland lately. Just be careful with him. I know he's useful."

"You know more of this world than I do, Alice of Wonderland," Tiger Lily said, getting up and leaving Alice with the book in her lap. "I will consider this. And I will continue to earn your forgiveness for my acts against you."

"Well, my wrist feels better," Alice said. "And my leg looks a lot better. You're off to a good start so far," Alice told her, smiling. She looked down at the red book and ran her fingers over the cover, nervous and a little uneasy about it.

She remembered saying something about this before. That bit about the red book had been in the brown book as a means to reverse the heart stealing. She'd already dealt with pages from this book before. Had she touched it as well? Or was this the first time?

"What did you do?" she asked Tiger Lily. "You said you did only bad things with this book. What did you do with it?"

Tiger Lily did not look at Alice for a moment. Eventually, she turned, Alice meeting her eyes and Tiger Lily taking a breath before letting the words come out. "There are pages about incense that will stop a person from leaving to other places. It works surprisingly well, though I wish it did not. It did not say you would fall so ill or that you would continue to try and leave."

"Oh."

"There is a way to stop any creature's heart. I have hunted and caught strange prey with that, though these are not proud moments. I tried it when they attacked my village, but the men Wendy brought did not have hearts to stop. I used the book once to try and heal. I am not as good as my sisters. What I tried only made the suffering worse."

She fell quiet for a moment, thinking of what else to say. Alice waited patiently, knowing better than to interrupt. Tiger Lily had suffered and she was still so much stronger than Alice ever could hope for. When Tiger Lily straightened again, Alice was still listening.

"The Cheshire Cat would often ask me to read the book for him," she said. "He said that it would be a way to help my people if I could read the book, but I have not trusted it since. It is like the one Wendy has and that is an evil thing. I have refused, but still he asks. And then he said that I could give it to another who might read it for him. I have chosen differently. Like you, I am learning quickly not to completely trust a cat."

"Tiger Lily?" a voice from outside called into the tent. Alice's heart caught in her chest at the sound of it. She hadn't heard that voice in almost a year now, but she knew one that was very similar to it. "Are you talking to that cat in there again?"

The flap opened and he walked in, tall with dark hair and looking much like he did before, except in clothes that fit a lot better in Wonderland. He looked between the two of them and stopped when he saw Alice. Adam Case was right here and Tiger Lily knew the whole time.

"You found him and you didn't tell me?" Alice demanded. She tried to get up, though a shot of pain made her wince. Tiger Lily went back to her side and helped her get to her feet. "How long have you known about him?"

"Is this one of the two you were looking for? He said that

he was not familiar with you, Alice of Wonderland. I think perhaps he was lying to me."

"Adam, what are you doing here?" Alice demanded. She let go of Tiger Lily once she was upright and turned on him, trying not to put too much weight on her leg. "You've been missing for almost a year. I have looked *everywhere* for you and you were nowhere."

"Since when do you call me Adam?" he asked.

"I spent Christmas at your house." She let out a breath. She should be happy. She'd finally found him. "It has been a really long year. But you're back! I can bring you back to school and then I just need to find Matt and I'll be done. It can't take me more than another year to find Matt, right? Please tell me you know where he went."

"I hate to break it to you," Adam said, "but I'm not going back yet. I've still got some stuff to do. Hearts to steal. Robin Hood of Hearts and all that."

"*No*," Alice told him. "You're going to come back! What is with you guys? Mike did the same thing and I had to get him airlifted out of the castle with a dragon before he'd finally leave the castle and go home. I am *not* doing that again. You don't *need* to do anything here except come home."

"Are you from this place she speaks of?" Tiger Lily asked, looking like she was also growing suspicious of him. "And it is a home you can return to. Why do you not go with her? She has been looking for you for a very long time."

"I'm not done here yet," Adam said, backing away from the two girls. Tiger Lily looked like she was going to pounce on him at any moment.

"He has a family back home," Alice told her. "A sister and many brothers and a father. None of them know where he is. Well, one of them kind of knows. I had to rescue Mike — Lance — one of you from the Queen of Hearts already."

"But he's fine, right?"

"He is a pain in the ass, but fine," Alice told him. "And your sister's seeing a nice boy named Wyatt."

"Lance is slipping," Adam muttered.

"Just come back with me," she said, letting the desperation creep into her voice. "I don't have much time to get you and Matt out of here before you're going to be stuck here forever. There's just one year and then I can't get you out of here anymore, so plea — *ah!*"

Alice grabbed her head as that knife in her mind twitched and moved. Extra things poked at the edge of it and she could feel something tearing. She lost her balance and fell backwards, Tiger Lily diving down to catch her before she could hit her head. Alice's eyes stayed open as she went down, though she could see nothing for that moment except the crack in the world at the edge of Wonderland, dark against the bright light.

"You seem busy," Adam said, slipping out of the tent in the moment of confusion and Tiger Lily let him go, getting Alice back to the bed as the vision passed over her.

Alice let out a groan as it stopped, glaring out the flap and trying to catch her breath. "Sorry," she said to Tiger Lily, sure to look her in the eyes when she did so. "I don't know what happened."

"I have seen it happen to Peter before," Tiger Lily said. "He has said there is a hole in his brain. I suggested perhaps he be quick enough to not get shot next time."

Alice smiled, but that didn't help her. "I don't know what's going on anymore," she said, her mouth still smiling but she could feel the tears of confusion welling up in her eyes. "I didn't even want to come back here. I thought I just had to get Adam and Matt back, but I think everything is so much bigger than that now. Maybe it always was. I don't want to do this anymore, Tiger Lily."

"You said you had one year," Tiger Lily said, searching her eyes and desperation before pressing onwards. "Why do you have one year to find them and remove them from Wonderland?"

"Because the Bandersnatch is going to take me after that," Alice told her. "I made a bet with him that I can't win. I traded him the only hope I had to maybe come up with some way to beat him, and now he's going to take me away when I finish middle school."

Tiger Lily looked on with worry and confusion, Alice looking down and trying to breathe deep and regain her composure so she wouldn't start to cry. "It has been a very, *very* long year," Alice said. Her voice was hollow and defeated, but she pulled the red book into her lap again and let her fingers run over the cover. There was no way out for her, but she could hope that there was some way to get the boys out before she disappeared.

"I have to get them out. I owe it to Adrianna. It's my fault they're in here. I'll send them back, then the Bandersnatch will take me. It will all be over."

"You will find another way, Alice of Wonderland," Tiger Lily said, laying a hand on Alice's back.

Alice took a deep breath, pushing back those dark thoughts. She still had a year before she would be falling victim to the Bandersnatch. And she had found Adam, though she wasn't able to make him come back over. Yet. And at least he still had his heart and he looked well. He even seemed fine with Alice there, not at all surprised to see her though she was shocked to see him. Next time she wouldn't shout. Next time, she would find a mirror, slip it under his feet and drop him back at school.

Progress was made this trip. For all the bad, there was still progress.

"I think someone came through from Neverland," Alice said suddenly, realizing what that feeling in her mind was. Someone made the hole bigger and got through. She didn't know who or what, but she was hoping desperately that whatever it was, it wasn't dangerous. She hoped, at the very least, that it was alive.

"Perhaps you should close it, then," Tiger Lily said. "Wonderland is no place for Neverland. Neverland is no place for Wonderland."

"It would strand everyone in Neverland."

"They should not know of Wonderland," Tiger Lily said firmly. "This is a strange place that we have invaded. It will suit them poorly and they will likely starve here as my people are doing should they come through. They will not learn to survive and they will perish. It is crueller to let them through to die slowly than leave them there to die quickly."

"I don't even know how I'd do it," Alice said, though already she was trying to think of a way. It was just like icing over her mind, with a knife stabbed in, ready to take a slice. Or a hole where the knife had been. Alice tried mentally pulling some of the icing over, spreading it across where it was missing and gradually covering the large hole left in the icing of her brain. She had no idea if it did anything, but by the end of it she was exhausted and already lying down to sleep.

ALICE WOKE THIS time to Tiger Lily over her, trying to wake her up. A thought had suddenly occurred to Alice. She clapped her hand over her wrist and brought the watch up to look at, only to have it drop off her wrist into her face. She picked it up and looked.

It was Monday morning. Six in the morning. She had been gone the entire break.

"I'm going to be late!" she said, grabbing her bag and vanishing. "Thank you for everything, Tiger Lily!"

CHAPTER 15

And Back Again

ALICE ROLLED OUT of the mirror and landed with a loud thud and a groan of pain. Her leg was not suited for rolling right now. She had to be quiet, what with the sun not even thinking about coming up just yet. She tried her best to stifle the groan of pain and to hobble up to her feet, but found herself unable to quite make it.

The light came on and Alice was not expecting the sight she saw. Adrianna sat up on her bed fully alert, but there was also a nest of blankets on the floor and Mike standing at the door, hitting the light switch and wiping the sleep from his eyes.

"I told you she'd be back." Mike said, going back to his blanket nest.

"Alice!" Adrianna said, throwing herself on Alice in a hug and Alice wincing at her weight. "I was so worried. You weren't here when I got back and I know you were planning to go off for the week but I thought you'd be back by now. What happened?"

"A lot," Alice said honestly as Adrianna lifted herself off of her. Both she and Mike noticed the leaves and splint on Alice. Mike came to her side and helped get her to her bed to sit and to put her leg up. "It's not that bad anymore," Alice assured them both. "It used to be a lot worse. And I think my wrist is better."

Alice started to peel the leaves off of her wrist. Sure enough, it had healed completely. "I didn't miss anything, did I?" Alice asked, continuing to carefully peel back the leaves. "I know I was gone a little longer than usual."

"No classes yet," Mike said. "What the hell happened to you?"

"Neverland. Neverland and Peter Pan. There were zombie wolves. It's not important."

"You didn't get bit, did you?" Mike asked, suddenly a lot more worried.

"No," Alice said. "Why?"

"Zombie bites… you haven't seen a zombie movie before, have you?" He had become familiar with Alice's complete lack of understanding anything relating to pop culture over Christmas and he looked very tired of it. "Just — never mind. What were you doing there this whole break? I thought you were going home."

"Something came up and my parents wanted me to stay here," Alice said. "So I decided to go looking for Adam and Matt in Wonderland again. Oh! And I found Adam! That jerk's been avoiding me while I was there, I think. And he just ran off when I tried to get him to come back."

"You should probably expect that," Mike said.

"I thought *one* of you would be sensible," Alice said. "It isn't safe in Wonderland. And apparently he said something about being the Robin Hood of Hearts, which if that means he's breaking in and he's the one stealing the hearts and giving them to everyone, he's going to get caught. It's a miracle he hasn't gotten caught yet."

"You're going to have a hell of a time getting him out of there," Mike told her. "It sounds like he's found people to save. Or people he needs to pay back. Or get payback on. He isn't going to want to leave until he's done. You should probably just leave him until he gets it all sorted out. I mean, you know where he is now, right? It won't be that hard to track him down again."

Alice glared at him. "You are not helping," she said, slowly taking the splint off to see how bad her leg was. "At least I have Tiger Lily helping me. She said that if she saw him, she'd keep tabs on him and make sure I could find him again and bring him back when I go back there next time. Which might not be for a while," Alice said, wincing as she got the rest of the splint off.

Her leg was a patchwork of bruising under the leaves. Where her wrist was completely healed, her leg looked like it was still freshly injured. It was a mess of yellows and blacks and purples and reds, like the ugliest painting she had ever seen. It was no wonder at all that she was in so much pain when she walked on it. She needed to get it properly treated. "I am not going to go back there for a while. Not until this heals."

"What did you do to it?" Adrianna asked, looking horrified at how bad it was.

"I think I fell down a hole," Alice said. "It's a little fuzzy, that part. I'll tell you all about it, but I think I'm going to need a hand down to the nurse. I should get this looked at properly. There's only so much leaves can do, right?"

Adrianna and Mike helped her up before Mike opted to just carry her down. They went slowly so as not to jar the leg. Adrianna stayed at her side, ready to corroborate whatever story they came up with as an explanation.

"Just say you fell out of bed," Mike told her.

ALICE SPENT THE next several weeks with her leg

wrapped tightly and walking on crutches with few questions asked. She laughed, saying that she'd fallen out of bed, and the nurse that night did not ask anything else. Instead, she wrapped it and gave Alice a note for missing her first class, telling her to stay off of it for the next few weeks.

That was fine by Alice. It gave her a fine reason not to go back to Wonderland and spend her evenings deciphering the brown book's notes. Between the mattress where it used to be, Alice kept the red book, not ready to delve into that one just yet. There was still so much that she could pick up from the rest of the book that she knew would come in handy if she just spent a little more time with it.

It wasn't until much later that Heather came to her looking distraught. "Alice, I'm so sorry!"

"Sorry?" Alice asked. "For what?"

"Nike!" she said. "Alice, I'm so sorry. I tried to talk her out of it — like, she *knows* you guys are dating — but she thinks she's in *love* and apparently you 'Can't steal your true love,' or some crap like that." Heather rolled her eyes, annoyance and sympathy battling on her face.

It took Alice a moment to remember Nike in the first place. Right, the boyfriend she didn't want. She hadn't seen him since coming back from the break, but it was nice that she wasn't going to have to deal with him anymore. It sounded like he'd found someone else. She looked to Adrianna instead, who was the whole reason she was going out with him, but Adrianna looked sympathetic towards her as well.

"Oh," Alice said, not really upset at all, though it seemed everyone else was upset for her. "Well, that's too bad," she said, getting back to her homework. "Solves one problem."

Kevin smiled, but Heather was crushed. She looked like there was something more to it, but whatever it was, she didn't say. "Ice cream and girly movies," Heather offered. "Best way to heal a broken heart."

"No thanks," Alice said. "We have finals. And you guys have the play. We don't have time to take a night off, right?"

Heather hugged her tight, but she let the matter drop after insisting that if Alice change her mind, she was there for her.

They went to see the play that weekend, Alice realizing only then that Adrianna was strangely unaccompanied. They went as a group and hung around afterwards to tell Heather and Kevin how awesome they were, when Alice saw Nike in the hall with his new girlfriend. She was taller than Alice, blonde as well and laughing at his jokes.

Sarah. That was Sarah next to him.

Alice stared at her, her mind racing as she tried to make sense of it. Sarah, who had been taken by the Bandersnatch, was here. It wasn't just a girl who looked like her. The laugh was the same, and those eyes, and the way she carried her-self. She was trapped in a statue, so how was she here now?

The Bandersnatch wouldn't have just let her go without reason.

"Alice," Nike said, sounding intentionally casual as he did. "I almost didn't see you there. How was your break?"

"It was okay," Alice said on her crutches. She kept staring at Sarah.

"Adventure?" he asked, nodding to her knee, still wrapped tightly with a bandage.

"You could say that," she said. Even up close, she couldn't understand how Sarah could be standing right there. Was she real? "Hey Sarah. How've you been?"

"*Mine* went very well," he said, puffing up his chest and smiling wide as he looked over all of them. "We went and saw so many shows and had a lovely time. And I met Sarah, here. It turns out we have a lot in common and we hit it off right away."

"That's great," Alice said. Something was off. Something gnawing at the back of her mind.

"Say," Alice said, tearing her eyes off of Sarah to Nike, "how's Wyatt?"

Nike's eyes went wide and he shrank away. It was like the mention of the name scared him, which it shouldn't. Every time they'd gone out was with his roommate. It was strange that he wasn't here, and that Adrianna hadn't been spending time with him.

"Well, look at the time," he said, looking at his watch. "We better go, Sarah. We don't want to miss curfew." They left her, walking a little too quickly away.

She didn't say a word, but Alice could tell that was Sarah. She was different now, but it was still her. The Bandersnatch had let her go and she was too stunned to put together what that meant. She didn't have to rescue her anymore, but it didn't stop there…

Robert shook his head and patted Alice on the shoulder. "I still can't believe she went and did that to you. I don't know what you said to them, but you got them running," Robert said, sounding a little proud of her.

"I just asked him about Wyatt."

"Who?" Adrianna asked.

Alice looked at her for a moment. Nike was scared when she mentioned it and Adrianna was unaccompanied by Wyatt. It made sense, but she couldn't quite figure out why. But she was out with friends and could not dwell on this any longer. Alice smiled and waved it off. "Long story," she said. "I'll tell you later."

They didn't have to wait much longer before Kevin and Heather appeared from backstage with the rest of the cast to cheers from those who remained in the lobby. Alice was fairly certain the only people left at this point were friends and family. Alice saw that Kevin's father had even managed to show up, along with his mother.

Their group went to Heather first and let Kevin have the time with his family. They would have the rest of the week and all of finals to tell him he'd done a great job. Heather's one death scene was well done and they all told her so, though she insisted on being modest and telling them every little piece of the performance that she had gotten even the slightest bit wrong. She was thorough, but they did not let her get too upset with herself about any of it. It was opening night and there were little flubs everywhere that no one noticed. If they were flubs at all.

They migrated to Kevin once there seemed to be a break between his parents for them to come in. "Are these your friends?" his father asked, looking all of them over and nodding in approval at them.

"Robert, my roommate. Heather was in the play with me. And these are Adrianna and Alice. And this is my father and mother," Kevin said, indicating each of them separately.

"Hello," he said, smiling with pride down at Kevin. "Did you all enjoy the play?"

"It was great!" Heather said. "I still want to know where he learned to do all of that."

"Oh?" his father said, looking slowly back at Kevin with

his eyebrows raised and a mischievous smile on his face. "Did Kevin not tell you?"

"Please don't."

"Oh, but you were so good!" his mother said.

His father smiled, laughing a little to himself and grinning back at Kevin before looking back to them again. "While it would give me *never ending* joy to reveal it, my lips are sealed. I will say I approve of this much more, though."

Kevin watched his father and mother depart, leaving him behind to deal with his friends and their curious stares after them. Kevin shrugged it off and faced them dead on with a dark stare. With his makeup still on, he looked more serious than usual about it. "Don't ask."

Heather was not deterred. "I *will* find out," she promised him. "You have to let something about this dark secret past of yours slip out eventually."

"I really don't," he told her. "And if Robert snooping through all my stuff the last few months because you asked him to hasn't found it yet, then you're definitely not going to find out."

"You knew?" Heather asked.

"I never did it," Robert told her. "I'm not spying for you."

Heather looked a little defeated as they went back to the dorms, walking in their cluster and re-enacting their favourite parts of the play as they went. They had to move a little slower for Alice, who was getting pretty used to the crutches now, but she still ended up trailing at the back of the group.

"There is no way you just fell out of bed and did that," Heather told her quietly, dropping back to walk next to her. "Look, if you need it, I will punch someone in the face for you. I'm getting pretty good at it."

Alice laughed. "I think I'll be fine. But... Sarah?" She didn't even know what she wanted to ask, her mind still working circles around having seen her at all.

"Yeah, I could deck her. And then we'll do movies."

"No, I didn't—"

"I *told* her to tell you herself," Heather insisted.

"It's fine, Heather," Alice insisted. "Really, it's okay."

"I don't know what's with her. It's like everything's normal and one day she's completely different. There's no way Nike is that amazing, no offense. It's like there's nothing but Nike now. Since we got back, she's been doing nothing but hanging off of him. I kinda want to deck both of them, honestly."

"Maybe focus that on the play." Alice smiled. It was nice to know Heather was watching out for her, but she wasn't about to ask that of her. "You've still got a week of dying to finish."

CHAPTER 16

One Last Trip

THE SUCCESS OF the play was soon overshadowed by the dread of finals, which passed with as much anxiety and as many late nights studying as it always did. Alice was happy to actually join them in the madness this time around, though she was even happier to be off her crutches. Her knee was still bruised and difficult to walk on if she was up for too long, but she didn't have much reason to be moving around too much right now anyway. Everything she wanted to see kept coming to her.

Sarah was very easy to keep an eye on. Nike kept showing up wherever Alice was with Sarah in tow, staying in view but not so close that Alice felt the need to speak to him. Sarah had eyes for no one else, staring at Nike and barely looking down at her work. She seemed healthy and unmarked by her time with the Bandersnatch, if completely obsessed with Nike now. She was different, but she was back.

Which left Alice with many questions. Alice needed to know what was going on, and she knew just when she could slip away.

This was the second year that Alice would miss the year end formal, but she insisted that everyone else go have fun without her. Her leg would not agree with a night of dancing and she did not want to go if she wasn't going to be able to have fun. Heather looked at her sympathetically, like she knew what Alice was really doing, but they did not push her to join them.

Alice waved them off and waited until they were completely gone before she stepped out into the forest.

Walking through the underbrush was an unpleasant experience, but Alice managed it. Her limp returned, but she pressed on. She managed to hobble her way into the dome of fog and out the other side to much more solid ground.

Alice wondered if perhaps the Bandersnatch was colorblind. The whole area was in shades of grey now, shining in parts and dull in others. There were little silver trees that were growing through his garden which, thankfully, only seemed to have two new faces this time in it. She saw Wyatt standing where Sarah had been and another older boy who looked rather resigned and sat on his pedestal where the rest stood.

The pressed dirt beneath her feet was a welcome change as she made her way through the garden, looking through the domain of the Bandersnatch. There were, she noted, touches of obsidian so dark she could see herself in it amidst the overwhelming amount of silver. There was also a good amount of glass sprinkled in here, but nothing seemed to be alive. She wondered if that was because he wanted to make sure people knew just how alone they were when they came in.

"You let her go," Alice said, feeling the shadow over her as she looked up at Wyatt. He looked so confused and scared. More confused. "It's like she doesn't remember being gone at all. Like she's someone else almost. But she's not."

"Yes, that one was interesting," the Bandersnatch said, appearing next to Alice as a black formless shape. He settled down into something of a wolf or a bear next to her, black with no features but those four eyes looking at the statue that was Wyatt. "The boy wanted you to love him, but we have a standing bet and I rather enjoy watching you try to figure it out. He then asked for a girl that would make you jealous. He selected that one in exchange for his friend. In a way, he saved your friend."

"But why doesn't she remember?" Alice asked, turning to the Bandersnatch. "Evan remembers. Why doesn't she?"

"She will," the Bandersnatch said. "He wanted her for his loving and devoted girlfriend. When he tires of her, she will remember. You would have enjoyed watching him as he realized that she was once his classmate. He'd selected a girl he didn't realize he knew. He wanted to rescind our arrangement. And now you have no one in my garden you are loyal to left to release should you win our little bet."

Alice hadn't thought of that. Besides Wyatt, who she really didn't know that well, there was no one left here for her. She'd seen some of these faces before, yes, but she knew none of them and had no drive to save them.

"But now I don't have to save her anymore," Alice said. She was almost relieved about it. It was one more person off of her list of people to rescue. Where the Bandersnatch seemed disappointed that she wasn't more troubled by it, Alice was relieved. With Sarah already saved and Adam found, she was down to Matt before she was done.

"I hope you will still find some reason to continue with our little bet," the Bandersnatch said. "You still have everything to lose, even if you have nothing to gain. And you have not even tried to do anything to convince me, yet. Oh, I do wait for the day you try to convince me to leave."

Alice felt a prick at the back of her mind, like someone was getting through again, and mentally covered it up with that icing. She was running low and she worried she wouldn't have enough to last. It was spread so thin already.

"You've redecorated," Alice said, turning away from Wyatt to look at him. She winced as her foot hit an uneven patch of ground, though she tried not to let the pain show on her face. "You're just missing the floor now. Maybe the stone. It would go with everything else you have going on here."

"Alice, if you wish for sympathy, you must find it in a more genuine sense," the Bandersnatch said "You have the means to fix that leg on your own and will get no more from me."

Alice was about to ask what he meant, but she was back in her room a moment later, lying on her bed with her leg propped up as she was supposed to be for the evening. Beside her on the bed was the red book. She glared at it, shaking her head. The Bandersnatch was trying to have his fun before he took her away forever.

She picked up the red book and felt it pulsing under her fingers before she opened it. It was powerful, possibly more so than the brown book. Granted, the brown book lost some of its power when she released the Bandersnatch and the Jab-berwocky and the jubjub birds. She wondered if there was something inside this book as well that waited to be let out.

Gently, she went through the book. It was not fragile under her fingers, but she worried that it might snap at her if she handled it too roughly. She moved through it a few pages at a time, just trying to get a general idea of what was in it and little else.

It looked like a biology book, but one the likes she had never seen before. It was about repairing and destroying bodies, piece by piece. She skipped quickly over the section about hearts, but it mentioned organ after organ after organ. It was more broad at the beginning, but as she got further into it, the detail grew.

The second half, as with the brown book, was much more practical. It broke from information about the pieces of the body and outlined the various things you could do with them. There was something to hold a body still and keep it from moving too far, and variations on it for different physical make ups and abilities. She found a bit about those who could move through places and the special things you did to hold them there in a part that had been clearly read several times over.

She found more and more in here, mostly healing with a little on the reversal of it. It was more about healing, though. The holding spells were to keep a patient still for other procedures, though there was plenty in here that could be used for harm as well.

Alice stopped after half an hour, putting her thumb in the book to hold her place and then listening to the music from the dance wafting in from the window. She shouldn't be looking through this alone. Without Adrianna here, she wouldn't know if she was losing her mind like the Queen of Hearts had. Or Wendy had. And what would be more interesting to the Bandersnatch's game than having an insane hero trying to take him down?

Putting the book back under the mattress, she looked around the room. Her eyes fell on the mirror and she shook her head. Now that she had the evening, she had something else that she should really be doing. Getting to her feet, Alice went to the mirror and brought up Tiger Lily's teepee.

Her watch was missing. Though she looked, it was nowhere on or in her dresser. She hadn't seen it since she had been at Tiger Lily's last and she hoped it was still there. If not, she would just have to be careful to make this a quick trip.

She felt something poke at the inside of her brain as she passed through the mirror. It didn't sting like someone passing through Wonderland, instead it feeling a bit more like a light nudge. It was strange, but not painful, and she ignored it.

It wasn't until she was standing in front of Tiger Lily's tent that she realized there was no way to knock. Alice stood awkwardly for a moment at the opening, wondering if she should just walk in or call for her. She didn't know the proper etiquette for a tepee set up in a field.

"Have you forgotten how to enter?" Tiger Lily asked behind her.

Alice jumped and turned to face her. "There you are! I thought you might be inside. I... do you knock?"

"Knock on what?" Tiger Lily asked, opening the flap for

Alice and letting her in. "You have been gone a long time, Alice of Wonderland, and still you do not walk right. Are your healers not as skilled?"

"Not here to talk about that," Alice said, looking around for some sign of her watch. "You said you would look out for Adam. Have you seen him?"

"He is as difficult to find as you," Tiger Lily said, looking disappointed in herself. "I know what he does. The Mad Hatter stole many hearts and let the owners of those hearts take them away. The Queen of Hearts has been catching them again. Adam has been going after these men. He says he can find you when you appear and sends the people to you."

Alice thought on this a moment, realizing what happened. He had found her. The spell had worked and time and again he had found her. He just never came out, instead sending the people of Wonderland out to her. And he thought he was doing a good thing.

Alice was going to drag him back by his hair if she had to.

"That figures," Alice said, keeping her expression blank. "Do you know where he might be?"

"I am sorry," Tiger Lily said. "He moves and disappears. I have seen him shrink away to nothing. He will return later, as if he was never gone at all. I do not know how he manages to do it, but he appears to eat something before he vanishes."

"Oh does he?" Alice said. She knew exactly what was

going on now and that gave her something to go on. "Thank you, Tiger Lily. You have been very helpful."

"You know where he is."

"I know what he's doing," Alice told her. "If you find him, you'll want to carry a jar with you. He'll become about small enough for that."

"You are going to find him."

Alice nodded. "Before I do, though, have you seen my watch? I think I dropped it when I was here."

"The small black device?" Tiger Lily asked. "It has been taken. I apologize again."

Alice smiled and waved her off. "No need. I'll find it. You've been a great help, Tiger Lily. Thank you."

Alice waved and left the tent, her mind on the watch. She reached forward and took a step. That watch had to be somewhere in Wonderland. She wasn't sure who would steal such a thing from Tiger Lily, though she was pretty sure the only one who cared at all about clocks in Wonderland was the Mad Hatter.

Her hand was on a wrist when she reappeared. The arm jerked and Alice tumbled forward. They both fell to the ground, Alice looking up to see Adam there. He was as surprised to see her as she was to see him, dropping a small bag holding a few hearts that continued to beat as they spilled out onto the ground.

Adam reached for his pocket, pulling out a small vial. Alice let her hand disappear off of her wrist and pulled it out of his hand. He looked at his hand, then to the bottle in Alice's now attached hand. He reached into another pocket and pulled out a mushroom, which Alice snatched away as well and tossed over her shoulder. He tried grabbing things out of other pockets with both hands, but Alice's hands were already waiting and plucked the newest items out of his grasp.

"Stop!" Alice said, smacking him over the head with one of the items. She looked down at it, seeing the White Rabbit's fan. No, there was no time to feel nostalgic. She focused on Adam. "Stop running away. Just stop that and talk to me!"

"Okay," Adam said, sitting down on the forest floor. "Hi Alice. How have you been? Leg feeling better?"

"Oh, you know," Alice said. "Running around Wonderland looking for these guys I managed to get trapped in here. Apparently none of them want to come back with me even though one of them has been following me around for months now. He never even told me that he knew I was looking for him. Kinda rude, don't you think?"

"I can explain," he said, reaching into his pocket. Alice snatched up the cake before he even had it out in his hand. "You're a little too good at that."

"Will you come back?" Alice asked desperately. She was

going through everything she could think of right now to slip beneath him and make him go back anyway.

"When I'm done," he said.

"You aren't in debt to the Mad Hatter too, are you?" Alice asked. "Mike was and he made me rescue him with a dragon before he'd come back with me. You know it's been a year, right?"

"It can't be a year."

"Look at the watch," Alice said, nodding down to it. "That's accurate."

"It doesn't even move," Adam said. "I've watched it and it doesn't do anything. And it pokes a little on the strap, you know. I have to wear my shirt under it."

"A watched clock will tick no more than a watched pot will boil," Alice told him. "Especially not a digital clock in Wonderland. Look away, look back and it will give you the newest time. I promise you, that's how I've been making sure that I'm not gone too long and no one misses me. Come here," she said, grabbing him by the wrist and taking a look at the time. Everyone would be back and in bed by now.

"Adrianna's going to be worried," Alice muttered. Though Adrianna would figure out where she'd gone eventually, Alice hadn't left a note.

"Then just go back," Adam told her. "I'll be fine here."

"You know Matt's still in here somewhere too, right?"

Alice asked. "I have no idea where he is. I've found you and Mike by accident, but Matt's still out there somewhere and I have no idea where he is. Have you even tried to look for him in all of this?"

"Matt's fine," he said, brushing it off. "He's probably found a few people to terrorize and he'll be happy."

"He could be wandering around without a heart," Alice told him. "Might still be stuck in one of the walls of the castle. Did you think of that? Maybe he was sent out somewhere. I hear the Queen is planning to march a bunch of people off into Neverland. And trust me, as awful as Wonderland can be, I've been to Neverland now. You don't want Matt heartless and walking into Neverland."

"You worry too much," Adam said. "Tiger Lily's watching the tear between Wonderland and Neverland like a hawk to make sure nothing gets close enough. And now you got her looking for him too, right? It'll be fine."

"What are you even doing?" Alice asked, looking back between him and the bag of hearts. "You know those are hearts, right? Living, beating hearts. Out of people. Who are now walking around Wonderland like zombies. What are you trying to do?"

"Put them back," Adam said. "There's too many people out there that don't have their hearts. I can't just leave them like that."

"Yes, you can," Alice said. "You have a life back home. And I'm not going to be able to take you back to it for much longer. You don't get it. You're going to be stuck here if you wait too long because in a year, I can't ever come back here."

"Are you going to keep putting the hearts back if I'm not here, though?" Adam asked. "You put them back if they walk into you, but you haven't done anything to find the hearts yourself and put them back. It seems to me that you need to keep me here to give you a bit of a push to actually do anything to help the people here."

Alice reached over and grabbed the cake he was about to eat, throwing it over her shoulder. "It's not my problem," Alice said. "I can teach someone else how to do it before I can't come back anymore."

"Teach me. I'll do it. And when you can't get back here anymore then I can... Wait, why can't you get back here anymore?"

"In a year, if I can't win my bet with the Bandersnatch, he's taking me away forever," Alice told him, keeping her eyes on his. "If anything happens and I have to stop going to Lucena Academy, I'll have even less time. I don't know how I'm going to win against him. He's a lot more powerful and he's stubborn. And I traded my only trick for a little more time. I need you to come back or I won't be able to get you back."

"That was a stupid idea," Adam said. "But I'm not going until you put all the hearts back."

"Who was nice to you that made you need to do this?" Alice asked, exhausted from the argument already. "Someone adorable, I bet. A little family of hamsters or something? With one of them missing a heart and you just really needed to put it back and you felt so bad that you needed to save everyone else?" Alice rose to her feet, frustrated as she started to pace with a bit of a limp. "You have no idea how much I've been going through to get you back and you're just going to sit there and tell me, 'No thanks Alice. I don't want to go back. I want to stay here and save all the creatures and you can go back and die without saving me! I never wanted to see my family again anyway!' "

She threw her hands up in the air and grabbed the mirror out of the White Rabbit's house. Pulling it down, she saw that Adam had gotten his hands on something and he shrank before her eyes. Alice brought the mirror down over his head as he shrank and rolled away. She felt nothing in her head, nothing slipping through the mirror at all. She'd missed.

"Adam you get back here!" she yelled into the forest. "When that watch hits next year, you're going to be trapped here! Forever!"

She let out a scream of frustration. So close. She was so close and he'd just slipped through her grasp. She didn't know what else she was going to do. She flipped the mirror over and went through her options. He wanted her to return the hearts. Not every heart had been set free, she knew, so he was going to be stuck here for a long time. And she didn't have the time to put the hearts back.

Still, he was wearing the watch. She could find him and make him come back eventually. And he might run into Matt now that he knew he was out there. Maybe she could wait and let him find his brother and get them both out at once. Or Tiger Lily could find him and put him in a jar for her to bring over when she was ready. She could find him again. She could get him out eventually.

That was enough for now. She was tired and needed to get back before she was missed too much. She stepped through the mirror and fell back through to her room. Adrianna was asleep and she didn't have her brother, but Alice didn't feel too bad about that right now. She knew where he was and she knew how to get him back. For once, everything was not hopeless.

Alice went to bed. Though this summer would be her last, she had less to worry about than ever. Things were starting to look up.

About the Author

TANYA LISLE IS a novelist from the Metro Vancouver, British Columbia, who has series littered across genres from supernatural horror to young adult fantasy. She began writing in elementary school, when she started turning homework assignments into short stories and continued this trend well into university. While attending Simon Fraser University, she developed an appreciation for public domain crossovers and cross-platform narratives. She has a shelf full of notebooks with more story ideas than pens lost to the depths of her bag. Now she writes incessantly in hopes of finishing all of them.

Thankfully, her cat, Remy, has figured out how to shut off Tanya's computer when she needs to take a break.

www.ingramcontent.com/pod-product-compliance
Lightning Source LLC
Chambersburg PA
CBHW021952050726
47495CB00023B/1868